BAD MAKES BAD

"**Bad Makes Bad** establishes Ilyn Welch as the master of the Dark Cozy. Weaving elements of folk-horror and amateur sleuthing in this brilliant follow-up to Signs of Pain, Welch pushes the boundaries of genre, sending Cherry "Bomb" Orozco and the rest of the Raptor Flats gang into another neighborhood mystery where community and friendship are the ultimate foils to the most sinister schemes."
> —**Dr. Edward Karshner**, Folklorist and Professor of English, Robert Morris University

"Ilyn Welch tangles malevolence and turmoil together creating a fraught novella in **Bad Makes Bad**. Cherry Orozco must unwind this ruinous knot that strangles the community she cherishes, strand by strand in her own indefatigable way."
> —**Rob D. Smith**, author of **Good-Looking Ugly**

ILYN WELCH

BAD MAKES BAD

a Cherry Orozco Mystery

In loving memory of
Jenie Soriano-Francoso.

1

THE WOMAN, WHO WENT BY SALEM, circled the Los Feliz neighborhood playground.

A kaleidoscope of preschoolers zoomed in, out and around the apparatuses, climbing stairs, descending ladders and screaming down slides. Hiding in child-size tunnels, many kids shouted through peepholes toward the surrounding benches where nannies cooled their heels. A few parents were in the mix, sipping coffee. Doo-wop track "Daddy's Home" amplified from a boombox atop a picnic table on the outskirts of all the hubbub.

The park had a tributary of sand reserved for quieter parallel play, where three-year-old Tilda had been deposited by her dad. She sat content, surrounding herself with mounds of sand cakes topped off with twigs and leaves. Tilda's father Kirk was engrossed in a speaker-phone conversation about investing in a startup. He too repeatedly, absentmindedly, circled the play area, passing Salem several times, unaware of her tall figure in gunmetal gray schlepping a black messenger bag. When Kirk's public discussion segued into "invite procurement" for a corporate tent at Burning Man, he stopped several paces away from Tilda. Kirk waved away two intimidated nannies and their strollers, sitting down on the bench they vacated. A fiberglass seahorse on a spring obstructed his view of Tilda.

"Are those castles?" Salem said, sinking into the sandbox near Tilda's play constructions, flowing skirt melting into the ground.

"I'm making cakes," the child said.

"Want to hear a story?"

"Okay," Tilda said, mesmerized by pretty Salem's unblinking green eyes, freckly nose and long jet-dyed hair.

"There once was a mommy," said Salem, taking a white, yet-to-be-inflated balloon out of her bag, "who had two babies. Her husband left her and the babies for another woman."

Salem paused to blow up the balloon. With each exhale, a ghost figure outlined in black grew larger on the balloon surface. She deftly tied a knot.

"The mother went crazy," Salem said to the enraptured little blonde, bouncing the ghost balloon around the sand cakes.

With black-and-blue nails, some layers of pigment chipped, Salem raked a long line into the sand.

"So the mommy drowned her babies in the river." Salem uttered two splash sound effects as she bounced the balloon atop the sand stream. "But then the mommy was sad, and forever she looks and cries for her dead babies."

Salem whimpered, exaggerating a sad face next to the balloon before emitting a low-pitched wail.

"Her name is La Llorona," Salem told a wide-eyed Tilda. "Can you say *La Llorona*?"

"Ya Rorona," Tilda whispered.

"Good job!" Salem said. "You get to keep the balloon."

In the distance a man peeked from behind a tree, jutting a "What's up" with his chin at Salem.

Salem gave the child the La Llorona balloon. "Plus I have another surprise for you. I'm going to put it inside one of your delicious, baking cakes. Close your eyes, and when I say *La Llorona*, you can open them and look for your prize."

Tilda clutched the balloon, eyes squeezed shut. Salem nimbly rose from the sand. She dug into her black bag, producing a barber's straight razor with a tortoise-brown handle, opening it. Her eyes lingered on the glinting edge. She closed one eye and held it level with Tilda's pert nose, like an artist measuring proportions. Salem shook her head, folded the blade up, returning it to her black bag. Her hand resurfaced, balancing on her palm a clear acrylic box, inside stacked with razor blades. Dispensing one, she carefully submerged the blade into a stick-covered sand mound at Tilda's back. Poised to depart, Salem leaned down behind the child's head.

"La Llorona," she said with a hiss, slinking away toward the man at the tree.

Tilda opened her eyes, releasing the balloon. It bobbed to her side as she began to dig into the sand hills in front of her.

"Dog-poop bags," Salem said to the man at the tree, barely slowing as money exchanged hands.

In a blink, she arrived at the park's edge, plopping another La Llorona balloon, filled with heroin, inside the pet-waste station. The buyer caught up behind her, frantically lifting the lid of the can, exposing a foul sea of blue plastic sacks. As he fished out his score, Tilda's pained, panicked shrieks made him, and everyone else in the park, turn to the playground to see her father finally respond to his child's distress.

The junkie turned, searching for Salem, but she had long vanished.

2

READING WEBSITE MISSION STATEMENTS gave Cherry Orozco anxiety. Funny thing, she was searching online for a mental health counseling center with a sliding fee scale, and each "About Us" section made her more and more dizzy.

She needed to talk to someone about her anger issues. And her sleep issues. In the shelter of her Raptor Flats home at 5 Meadowlark Lane, Cherry experienced a similar intense dream every night. She would be at a store, on the street, at her beloved Eve's Beer Garden, or touring the White House. Ultimately in each dream Cherry would grab ahold of a varying stylish female, twentyish to thirtyish, and slap her in the face repeatedly. Some were strangers, some were famous figures, like Ivanka Trump during a White House-tour dream, though Cherry had never been to Washington D.C.

One nightmare figure reappeared more frequently: Long-haired dark brunette, olive skin with freckles across the bridge of her nose. A slim beatnik femme fatale.

Who the hell is she? Cherry obsessed and struggled to identify the apparition.

"Well, the licensed professionals at the," she squinted at the computer screen, "Quaking Aspen Center on nearby Satchel Avenue ought to know."

3

THE QUAKING ASPEN CENTER'S intake forms were involving. Questions covered family health history, past physical and sexual abuse, drug use. Ethnicity? Latinx. Do you consider yourself a member of the Lesbian, Gay, Bisexual and/or Transgender (LGBT) community? Yes. Issues you wish to address in therapy? Bad dreams causing sleep disorder, PTSD, anger.

She rubbed her short, fuzzy hair at the nape of her neck, which ached from leaning over the clipboard. Cherry's eyes burned from diminished rest. Hours before, Ida, her retired mother and housemate, had wakened her from the terrible recurring dream.

"You were moaning loudly," Ida said, feeling Cherry's forehead. "And you yelled *witch*."

"Witch?" Cherry said.

"The only word I could understand. You kept saying *Yaga* too."

A Quaking Aspen intake counselor, Carol, finally called Cherry into a private office, which had vestiges of the former building occupant: Land, Sea, Life Insurance. Cheap refurbishing provided new industrial carpeting that reeked of formaldehyde; the fumes gave exhausted Cherry an instant headache.

The counselor processed her forms. "How about an insurance card and your ID? Although the programs are free, we like to have your info on file."

Cherry handed over her license and proof of barebones coverage through Affordable Healthcare Exchange.

Carol's eyes lit up. "That's great you have subsidized insurance."

After scanning, photocopying and returning the documents, Carol revealed the only opening for service was group therapy on Wednesdays at eleven a.m.

"It's free," said Carol, who stared at Cherry through Gucci-frame glasses, waiting for a commitment. She tapped the cheap graphite rug with a kicky espadrille also stamped with the Gucci logo.

With the display of rich possessions, Cherry figured the professional staff were pedigreed enough.

"A bargain," she said with grouchy sarcasm. "Sign me up."

4

THE FIRST GROUP THERAPY session made Cherry elated.

Entering the Purple Room, a windowless space designated for group counseling, she was met with quite a few dour faces. Emotionally hollowed-out casualties sat in a kidney-shaped arrangement of second-hand furniture. The only available seat was the middle cushion of a lumpy sofa. She was glad she wore comfortable black sweats and her soft faded *Reading Rainbow* tee.

A female outfitted in elegant earth tones joined the fray, rolling an office chair with her. "Welcome to Quaking Aspen's Group Therapy. I'm Dr. Lidia Grekov, Center Director."

The psychologist pushed her seat in between two clients, sat down and crossed her trousered legs. Exquisite burgundy loafers caught Cherry's eye. *A trend of the profession.*

"Let's go around the room with introductions as well as what issues you seek to resolve." Dr. Grekov smiled and tilted her French-twisted head of auburn hair to the mustachioed middle-aged man sinking into a stained easy chair at her right.

"Um, Ned Capini here." From his throat came a couple of gravelly coughs. "I'm a Teamster at a film studio. Taking Wednesday mornings off to be here."

Ned paused as Dr. Grekov removed her phone from her pants pocket. While glancing down at her phone, she circled a manicured index finger for Ned to continue.

"When I was eight." Ned stopped. Deep in his raspy larynx came a choke. "My younger brother died from the flu."

Ned broke down sobbing. From behind his chair, Dr. Grekov retrieved a tissue box and placed it on the arm, then resumed perusing the phone.

"I had the flu first. Then Pete got sick." The man gasped for air, then went on. "After the funeral, my family never talked about it. I feel they blamed me, and I blame myself."

Ned wept quietly. Cherry realized her jaw dropped. The other group members' faces were distressed and sorrowful. She looked for cues from the psychologist, who remained glued to her screen.

Cherry blurted out. "You're not to blame. You were a child, it was out of your control. Even if you were an adult, it would be out of your control."

Ned's crying slowed. He yanked a tissue out of the box, blotting it around his cheeks. "Still, I have guilt."

"This is group therapy already working," Dr. Grekov said, swiping at her phone, finally slipping it back into her pocket. "It can set up a version of the family dynamic, a version that can be more beneficial than the one that left us lacking, left us hurting."

Though Cherry didn't feel assured by the chilly doctor, the theory impressed her. Until the female next to her on the sofa broke the spell.

"So, it'll be on us? We're going to be doing the work, while you remain indifferent?" The young woman peered at Dr. Grekov through geeky black glasses and squared raven bangs. "On your phone? And what if our problem isn't family related? What if it's dealing with a work issue?"

Dr. Grekov shot back over her own slick tortoiseshell glasses, forcing a smile across nude-pink lips. "In my experience, our core is family. Yes, it is up to you, and you decided to try group therapy—what's your name?"

"Parvati."

"When it's your turn, Parvati, you can talk about your work problem."

"How exciting," Parvati said, more towards Cherry.

As if at a resort, Dr. Grekov relaxed an arm atop the chair Ned slumped in. "Who's next?" She looked blankly at a blond-to-the-eyelash man.

The man tugged at a tailored denim shirt, lowering his chin. "My name is Brian," he said robotically into the collar. "My mother has always hated me."

"Thank you, Brian," Dr. Grekov said. "Let's move on so everyone can speak."

Turning to Cherry, Parvati sucked in her freckled cheeks and rolled her eyes. Cherry held in a bubble of laughter, releasing the pressure by pretend coughing into her bent elbow.

5

"COOL SHOES." Cherry pointed to Parvati's thick-soled green creepers patterned with Frankenstein's face as they exited the Quaking Aspen Center.

"Thanks, Cherry. And I love your shirt," Parvati said. "'Take a look, it's in a book!' By the way, I don't think Dr. Loafer gives a shit about your slappy bad dreams."

Cherry let out a hoot, then laughed while slapping her own thigh. "That's rich! Dr. Loafer?! She must be rich. Those high-end shoes and clothes."

Parvati blew on chipped purple fingernails and rubbed them on a vintage button-down calico shirt, with a mock high-and-mighty face. "I like how she wanted to skip me because I spoke out of turn. Telling me, 'We're running out of time, Parvati.' What can we do? It's free therapy."

"Yep, fits my budget. For now, I feel like a million bucks compared to those other poor souls," Cherry said, semi-hushed. "At least until this evening's nightmare. I hope we all get better."

Brian walked past them, stiff as a board.

"He is so blond." Parvati shielded her eyes. "It hurts my pupils. See ya next week!"

6

AT HOME, IDA WAS GLUED to the news on TV. "How terrible."

"What, Ida?" Cherry said from the kitchen. She gave a final toss to seasoned vegetables and chicken on a baking sheet before sliding it into the oven. Being exhausted, her motor skills lapsed and she slammed the oven door, startling herself. Pressing the timer for 30 minutes, she joined her mother.

"What's terrible?"

Ida pointed to the television. "Someone is booby-trapping playgrounds with razor blades. Children are getting hurt."

"Did they catch the jerk?"

"No, no suspect yet."

7

CHERRY COULDN'T FORM WORDS.

Cornered on the floor of a closet, clothes obstructing her vision, a shadowy young female blocked Cherry in. Each time she tried crawling away, the girl would shove an open book in her face, the page showing a scary picture.

"Baba Yaga is going to eat you!"

Finally, Cherry whacked away the book, slapped her tormentor on the cheek, and screamed. "STOP IT! STOP IT!"

"Cherry, wake up!"

She sat straight up in her bed. Her arm flexed to hit whoever roused her, but it was restrained by firm, brisk arm rubs. Cherry's eyes opened onto her mom.

"FUCK! Not again!" Cherry pushed away Ida's motherly caressing.

Ida retracted her hands, her expression a mix of concern and offense. "Would you rather I didn't wake you?"

"I don't know, Ida. My fucking world is upside down with these shitty bad dreams haunting me."

Cherry threw off her pine-forest blanket and stomped to their Snow White-themed bathroom.

Ida tightened her robe lapels, sighing. "You don't have to take it out on me."

Over the toilet flush, she yelled back, "Looks like I am! If I can get back to sleep, I'll apologize in the morning."

8

"HEY, BOMB!" Jill Vaca called out while letting herself into Cherry and Ida's home, *Bomb* being a high-school-era endearment for Cherry that stuck. She sat down in the Orozco's sunny dinette to join them for breakfast.

"Ida, there is no sweeter potato than you," Jill said. She lowered her voice. "Have Cherry's sleep patterns improved?"

Ida stirred creamer into her coffee mug, which featured a photo image of her small dogs, Yarn and Ball. To Jill she mouthed *no*.

"Coffee, Jill?" Ida said. "Cherry made it quite strong."

"Right, you better dilute my madness with creamer," Cherry said in a huff as she flipped a buckwheat pancake.

"I'm not complaining, dear," Ida said.

"Wonder what's got you so fucked up?" Jill said, immediately sorry to have cursed in front of Ida. "Well, guess what? I stopped by Acme Descanso and picked you up some low-dose THC gummies with CBD. Our friend Stu recommended this product for sleep disorders."

Jill held up a package, brand name Haiku Dream.

"Remind me what Acme Descanso is?" Ida asked. "And Stu?"

"The pot dispensary in the industrial area that Cherry introduced to me. Stu works there."

"He's a good egg," Cherry said. "Helped me out a while back during the church trouble."

"I've already had two edibles," Jill said. "And I'm hungry for a hotcake."

With spatula, Cherry flung a pancake at her friend. Jill caught it lefthanded, stuffing it into her maw.

"Also guess what?" Jill said, garbling through her pancake chewing. "Remember that crazy goth chick Lana? I am pretty certain I saw her at the dispensary."

Cherry slammed down the spatula.

"No shit," Cherry said. "Did you speak to her?"

"No way! I mean, if it was her, she's still pretty hot. But I steer clear of psychopaths and devil worshippers."

"How weird." Cherry tranced on the batch of sizzling batter. "You know, I think that nutjob's appearing in these bad dreams that are driving me insane," she said. "But you're not 100 percent sure?"

"Well, Acme security was escorting her out, like she was trying to pull some crapola. That fits her reputation."

"That fucking bitch is bad history to me," Cherry said, a worsened mood causing her to violently hoist flapjacks. "Since kindergarten she kept bugging me for second chances, but it was always part of her sick mindfucks. Like when she gave me a homemade smoothie that I drank, and afterwards Lana told me she blended her," behind Ida's back she pointed to her crotch, mouthing the word *pubic*, "hair trimmings into it."

Jill wretched. "Beyond mindfuck."

"It makes me sad remembering poor little Lana Picasso,"

Ida said, then addressing Jill. "Her family life was the pits, and her mother disappeared."

"Remembering that bitch makes my blood boil," Cherry said, throwing the spatula into the sink so hard it shattered a jelly jar.

Ida clicked her tongue, chastising Cherry with a glare.

"I apologize!" Cherry bellowed. "I'll be with Pearl!"

Beelining to her room where a framed Janis Joplin poster graced the moss-green wall, she shut the door with a bang.

"I hope this phase passes soon," Ida said into her coffee.

Eyes on Mrs. Orozco, Jill nodded in agreement and popped another gummy square.

9

"COPYCAT, COPYCAT," Salem recited while wedging razor blades into the welded seams of playground equipment. "Who is best? Copycat, copycat, I will stab your chest."

The svelte young woman diligently concealed the sharp objects throughout the deserted park not long past six a.m. Soon enough, the Yeshiva School teachers would emerge from the nearby campus, leading their preschoolers in single file, each kid holding onto the colorful safety rope. Salem knew one adult, an Orthodox woman, would be pulling a cooler filled with yogurt and apple sauce cups.

Perched on a concrete bench, a crow cocked its head, studying Salem's movements. She whirled toward the bird, crying, "Caw!" It jumped backwards wisely, instinctively.

Beyond the crow lurked a young man in a white buttoned-up shirt and black pants. Two curls cascaded from his skullcap. Adjusting her messenger bag, Salem strode to where he stood, hidden from the street by hedges near a jogging track.

"Eww, is that Shlomo?" Salem said, stepping sensually close to the man, who drew back.

"Solomon," he said. "You know me."

"That's right, fucker, I do know all about you," Salem said, hissing. "And I will call you whatever I want, be it Shlomo, Solomon, fucker, or junkie."

Salem snapped her fingers, then turned her back to the man. Her palm faced skyward in the "down low" position.

"Lay a fat roll on me, or I'll tattle."

From his austere slacks, Solomon extracted it, indeed the fat roll of bills, concealed in the recesses of his hand. Salem accepted the transfer.

"Trash," she told him over her shoulder, leaving his side.

Away from the playground at the end of a sidewalk, Salem fished out a balloon. Before dropping it into a can buzzing with flies, she looked back at Solomon, stuck out her tush, and rubbed the white blob over her butt crack and crotch. Salem hurled the balloon into the garbage, wove among parked cars, disappearing down a street of Spanish-style apartment buildings.

10

CHERRY WRIGGLED AND SHIFTED on the lopsided couch cushion in the group therapy room. "I probably have PTSD from recent events. Had to testify in court, because I discovered a church-run adult day care in Raptor Flats was actually a front for a sex ring. The adults were developmentally disabled."

Ned groaned. "Horrendous."

"I read about that in *The Raptor Flats Siren*," said Tara, an African-American, older female group member. "Disturbing."

"It will always disturb me, of course. In court, the defense team attacked me, my work history, my personal life, my rage. It depressed me." She gauged everyone's reaction. "Now I'm struggling with these recurring dreams and sleep deprivation. I lash out at my mom."

Cherry paused, waiting for Dr. Grekov to give a prompt, a hint, any guidance. The counselor glanced up from her phone, smoothing gingham pants over her knees, and flexed a caramel loafer mule that flaunted a baby-smooth heel. Cherry thought of her own cracked-skin feet inside shabby sneakers, retracting them awkwardly.

Parvati shook her head and clicked her tongue at Dr.

Grekov. She opened her mouth to speak, but Tara got there first.

"Can you describe the dreams again?"

"Different scenarios, but I always end up slapping the face of a woman who is egging me on, laughs at me, scares me. When the dreams first started, I would yell in my sleep, my mom waking me. Then I'd take it out on her. Now when it happens, I realize it's a bad dream. I don't panic, but I wake up after the dream, unable to fall back into a healthy sleep." Cherry let her back rest on the sofa.

"The dream is so specific. It doesn't seem related to that church-crime ordeal," Tara said, twisting a strand of salt-and-pepper hair. "Can you think of any cause?"

Dr. Grekov tapped a fingernail on the chic frame of her glasses. "Very sharp, Tara. However, let's pick up with Cherry next time and move on to your concerns."

Tara looked down at the floor, her face melancholy and serious. "Mel, my close, longtime lady friend. Well, I'm about fed up."

Blond Brian raised his hand. "Isn't Mel a man's name?"

Cherry sat upright. "Does it matter?"

"It's confusing to me," Brian said.

"Mel is short for Melinda." Tara's voice sputtered. "For all of our long...friendship, Mel has always been the more outspoken. The more critical. Of me. And I'm tired of it. But after so many years invested, it would be so sad to...end it." Tara faced the doctor, who leaned an elbow on the armrest of her chair, thumb and forefinger supporting her unblemished chin. The counselor closed her eyes.

Parvati made a loud annoyed sigh toward Dr. Grekov. "Wow. Okay, let *me* engage with you, Tara. Is Mel your lover?"

Tara's eyes welled, and her lips folded inward. She struggled to express herself, trying not to cry, a case of hiccups taking over. "She's my companion," she said through a couple involuntary spasms.

Cherry sat at the edge of the bad sofa, leaning toward Tara, forearms on her knees. "Doesn't matter if your relationship is intimate or not. If Mel's treatment of you feels wrong, you need to get away. At least take a break."

Tara's hiccups slowed. Dr. Grekov stood up and kicked a tissue box out from under a chair with her dazzling shoe, sliding it toward Tara's feet. Parvati snatched it up, placing the box on the despondent woman's lap.

The counselor remained standing. "Some progress made, but our time is up. I'll see you all next week." She wheeled her chair out of the room.

As they walked out, Ned patted Tara's shoulder. "Chin up," he said. "We'll help you sort things out."

Parvati flashed a goofy smile to Cherry, holding her hand up for a high five. "Good advice."

Cherry clapped her palm, feeling a smidgen of triumph.

11

ABSORBED IN THE TELLY, Ida sat with Yarn and Ball snuggled at her slippered feet.

As she entered the living room, Cherry braced against the corridor wall. She huffed and groaned her way to the coffeemaker.

"Um, can I make you something for breakfast, sweetie?" Ida said.

"*Mmm mmm*," Cherry said. "I'll do it. Let me sip some java first, to wake up some more."

Mug in hand, Cherry shuffled to join her mother to watch the morning news.

"Any better last night?" Ida asked. "I didn't hear any noise."

"Eh. Unfortunately, my body's getting used to it. I wake from the same nightmares, knowing in my sleep it's a dream, but unable to change the channel."

Sinking back into the chair, Cherry slurped her caffeine, its effect opening her eyes beyond slits.

"I apologize for the impatience," Cherry said to her mom as they both faced the TV. "I will try to be less angry."

Ida audibly blew her daughter a kiss.

"Look!" Ida said, changing the subject, giving the news

report her attention. "That wacko is still at large, putting razor blades around city playgrounds."

"Again?" Cherry said, raising her voice at the screen. "Someone was doing that a few years ago, until they were caught. Fucking copycat. Makes my head throb."

Ida got up, causing the dogs to disperse, to massage her daughter's temples.

Cherry welcomed the care, relaxing her head back onto a Granny-square furniture cover.

12

SALEM WAITED, fetal curled on a marble slab, humming, moaning "Bela Lugosi's Dead" into the crook of an arm. Inscription on the connecting headstone read AT LAST, nothing more.

Footsteps scuffed through weed patches and dry leaves within the confines of the old burial ground known as Raptor Flats Cemetery. The movement ceased at a nearby plot.

Salem stayed put, humming.

"Psst!" It was a man, a customer, vibrating with expectant energy.

Ignoring him, she rose, sitting upright, facing the headstone. Salem emitted a low wail, rocking.

"Hey." The man stepped closer, reached toward her back, but stopped short of tapping.

In a flash, she whipped her arm around at him with a snap. "Back off, fuck face."

"Hold on, it's me, Juan. I'm here to cop. Don't you remember?"

She stood, looked down at the tomb, then at him. "I remember something," she said in a throaty crone voice. "And it makes me feel bad."

Salem froze, unblinking, staring at the confused chump.

Juan's mouth opened slightly, saying nothing. As he moved his hand to a pocket, Salem took a step toward him and shoved his chest.

"BAAAAAAD!" she shrieked in his face.

He clambered behind a gravestone, hugging it, peering around at her. "What the fuck?"

"What the fuck is right, dumbshit!" Salem kicked at his shielding stone. With the heel of her hand, she clobbered his shoulder repeatedly.

Juan tried to deflect the blows with his elbow. "Stop! What's your trip?"

"Why should I stop? Fucking lame-ass weakling. You're staying here. Because you neeeeeed me."

Salem socked him a few more times, then stomped around, kicking. Each kick at a grave marker coincided with a screech. With her thick shoe sole, she kept kicking at an eroded headstone. A small section at the embellished edge broke off. Picking up a walnut-size piece, she threw it at Juan, hitting his forehead.

"That fucking hurt!" Juan said, rubbing a section on his brow. He retreated toward three neighboring cemeteries—two Jewish, one Serbian—each separated by rusty chain. He sat under a tree on a memorial bench, watching Salem circulate the premises. *I should bail*, he thought. But he needed a fix.

The howling quieted, and Salem's gait changed: a lower, even glide, knees bent. Like Groucho Marx. For some reason Juan's hope for a transaction renewed.

She stopped a yard in front of him, posed in Groucho form, sure enough, eyebrows jumping under her bangs.

"Well, hello," Salem said, in character.

Confused, his face turtle-retreated. Juan turned around

to see if they had company. No one else in the Raptor Flats boneyard, but in the Serbian spread he saw a rooster. Then he spotted an old man. *Geezer must be hard of hearing, unaware of this crazy bitch's meltdown.*

Two Groucho steps closer, Salem spoke. "What you're gonna do now, ding dong, is put the bread on the bench."

Brightening, Juan got up quick. He removed money from his pocket.

He followed Salem's nod, placing the cash on the spot, sitting back down.

She slithered onto the bench right next to him, on top of the currency. Like the antics and assault never happened, she wiggled around, one hand rummaging under her keister. Salem leaned close to him while she stuffed the money into her messenger bag.

"You can have your balloon of shame after you...assist me with that old coot. Comprender?"

"Assist how?" Juan scratched his cheek.

Salem made a compact, one-two pugilist gesture, then whispered into his ear, staying cemented to him even as he recoiled and disgust overwhelmed his face.

The senior man donned a brimless gray cap. He placed a long-stemmed, purple star-shaped flower at the base of a marble grave topped by an Orthodox cross.

The intimate, old cemetery was quiet except for a flock of chickens pecking for bugs. The gentle crunches of their feet and a refreshing breeze were a comfort. The gentleman sighed, shoulders relaxing, body meditative among Kalevich family graves. The short, weathered cluster of headstones stood in the center of a historic Serbian resting ground founded in the early 1900s. With a few other graveyards, the Serbian Benevolent Society Cemetery shared a city block between an industrial zone and a hill of scrub. California Black Oaks and a freeway overpass provided plenty of shaded solitude.

A dirt clod out of nowhere imploded at his feet. Looking down at the pieces, then around, the Kalevich descendant saw no other breathing human in that cemetery. The flying object's impact even made the chickens run from the family plot. But in the tiny adjacent Leibowitz Family Cemetery, someone seemed to be in deep grief. Or dead?

Collapsed over a slab was a woman with dark hair, wearing dark, muted clothes. Was her back shuddering or was that a trick of the dappled light? Mr. Kalevich steadied a walking stick and cautiously approached the figure.

He stopped at the chain separating the memorial parks, observing the unmoving person.

"Are you all right?" he called. "Miss?"

The chicken scratches had ceased, but the wind whooshed past his ears. Holding the swinging chain, the man slowly lifted one leg after the other over the perimeter. Inching forward to the grave and the woman, he curved forward.

"Miss?"

Surging up from the grave slab, Salem turned to the old man, vampire spit-hissing, zombie arms high and hands clawed. She jumped, standing on the vault, hovering over him as he clutched his chest.

Salem lunged at him as he stumbled away. Continuing to hiss, she chased him around the tiny grave section, weaving in and out of headstones. The man struggled to breathe and run as she pursued him around a memorial obelisk a few times. He scurried in another direction. As he passed a tall headstone embossed in Hebrew script, Juan stuck out his foot, tripping Mr. Kalevich into the gravel.

The man groaned, disoriented.

Juan hesitated, but grabbed his victim by the collar.

"What is happening?" said Mr. Kalevich, head lolling.

Juan turned to Salem, expression pitiful.

"Weak." She darted forward, seizing the man's shirt from Juan's grip. She shook him hard, hissing then croaking then cackling. Taking the cane, she cracked the side of his head. Mr. Kalevich went limp, a trickle of blood on his temple.

Juan's dark-circled, sunken eyes watched Salem methodically take the unconscious man's wallet, watch and jewelry, wedding band included. His head hung. "Can I have it now?"

Salem stood, putting the loot in her bag. She took the good part of a cold-shoulder minute brushing off her clothes. Deadpan, she rummaged around in her sack. She held the white balloon, Juan's white balloon.

"It revolts me how low you just stooped for a motherfucking fix, you scumbag junkie." Salem held it teasingly, then threw the bundle into the other Jewish cemetery.

Looking for a moment at Salem, primal realization all over his face, Juan took off to find his score.

Salem scooped up a fistful of gravel, heaved it after him, shouting, "Dried piece of shit! I hope I never see you again! PENDEJO!"

13

SPRINGTIME WAS IN FULL FORCE with bright-blue skies and a temperature increase. Cherry pounded the sidewalks through Raptor Flats toward Eve's Beer Garden, the daylight bothering her bleary eyes despite shades and a bucket hat. Relieved to push through the door, she scanned around scores of women carousing about the bar or migrating to the patio. From an indoor booth, Zinnia Hudson waved long arms overhead. Cherry barreled over, sliding onto the rustic bench.

"Thank goodness you got a quiet spot," Cherry said, removing her hat, dropping the glasses into its upturned bucket. "How's the Department of Children and Family Services treating you?"

"Treating me fine with some days off, giving me a long weekend."

"I'm surprised to see your hair in braids. Very cute."

Zinnia pumped her palm under her tiny pigtails a couple of times. "Thank you. Last time we saw each other it was a short afro. What's taken so long?"

"Bad dreams, sleep interruption."

"Jill told me."

"Group therapy."

Zinnia motioned to a passing Eve's employee for three pints. "Pilsner, please." She refocused on Cherry. "Good for you! That church abuse case took a toll. PTSD."

"It's okay, and free. Most of the attendees are so wrecked, I come away from the session feeling better. Is that awful?"

"Sounds like it's working for you. Where is it at?"

"In the neighborhood, on Satchel. Quaking Aspen Center."

"Huh. Must be new."

Three shimmering beers were placed on the farmhouse table.

"Thank you," they said in unison.

The tavern music changed to an old blues tune. Zinnia closed her eyes, swaying her head and new plaits merrily, singing along to the words *Hoodoo Lady, how do you do?* They both grabbed the nearest mutual pint glass and clinked.

Cherry gulped and relaxed. "Too bad Jill's missing her song. Oops, well there she is."

Jill shimmied up to the booth, strutting in time to the song, lip-synching lyrics including the spoken line, "Boy, you better watch it 'cause she's tricky." She slipped behind the table, nabbing the third brew as if a holy chalice, drinking half in one breath.

"Thank you for requesting this song for me."

Pursing her lips, Cherry put one hand on her lower rib-cage, the other at her back, servant-bowing toward Jill. "'Twas a magical coincidence."

"Cherry was telling me her sleepytime woes, and that she's into group counseling," Zinnia said.

Nodding her black pixie haircut, Jill's face molded into a dopey but approving smirk. "Any hot girls in the class?"

"Don't be a classhole," Cherry said. "And not really. There's my buddy Parvati, a groovy dresser. Long black hair with square bangs, nerdy glasses. Straight."

Jill snapped fingers with a flourish. "Shucks. Speaking of black hair, what's the deal with Lana Picasso mixing pubic hair in your drink? Did you punch her?"

Cherry ruffled her buzz-cut hair manically. "No. She moved real close to me, smiling like an imp, daring me to lose it. She asked, 'Why are you mad? Can't you take a joke?' It was the same vicious cycle with Lana since we were tiny: We'd usually play her choice of twisted games. It would get weirder and weirder. She liked fighting and hurting. As a kid it was frustrating. I'd end up ghosting her."

Zinnia shook her head. "What a mess. I recall her going in and out of your life."

"Well, as kids we both loved books, dark folktales with witches and goblins in particular."

Jill laughed. "Warning sign!"

"Shaddup...I still love those stories. I recall some fun but brief times with Lana, us poring over the details in picture books. I had a couple books about the traditions and beliefs of a Mexican family, with intricate illustrations."

Jill smiled with a faraway look in her eyes. "I remember that book series from elementary school. It showed the abuela killing chickens for dinner. Realistic, but not gruesome."

Applauding, Zinnia chimed in. "I've seen those books when I visit county housing village libraries! Kids can connect and relate."

"I was fascinated by one page about the legend of La Llorona, Lana too, though she was way more obsessed with it. That devious bitch loved the book so much she stole it from me."

All three laughed, but Cherry became serious.

"One of the many times I stopped seeing her. This was the song-and-dance: She'd approach me with good behavior, as though she changed or matured. Maybe with an apology. I'd give her a chance. Then she'd fuck up. I finally stopped being gullible."

"What was the last straw?" Zinnia said.

Jill pounded the table. "I know this tale, but I want to hear all the gory details again!"

Cherry gulped her remaining beer. "We were in our late teens. Lana resurfaced after allegedly moving in with relatives in the Fairfax District, going to some fancy private school."

"Why did she move out of Raptor Flats?" Zinnia asked.

"It's murky, but I heard her mom died, and her dad disappeared. Or the other way around. Anyways, out of the blue she showed up at my door—long severe black hair, goth clothes, monkey boots—inviting me to see some band."

Jill clapped, grinned devilishly. "What was the band's name?"

"Oh, I found out after the fact—Jesus Christ Hated, a GG Allin tribute band."

Zinnia shook her head. "Remind me."

"A long-dead shock punk who would perform extreme acts, like shit on stage and throw it at the audience, and worse. But I didn't know that when I met her at the dingy club." Cherry waved for another round.

"Go on," Jill said.

"Why don't you tell it?"

Zinnia raised eyebrows and smoothed her braids. "Something bad happened, eh?"

"We stood in front of the stage, and a mosh pit exploded when the band began. Lana spat in the lead performer's face."

Zinnia's mouth fell open.

"Which is in keeping with that sick genre's *ideals*." Jill made finger quotes.

"The dude jumped offstage after her with a broken beer bottle. She pushed me to block him. I had to scuffle with him or he would have really fucked me up. I kicked the glass out of his hand and fought him off. He fell down kind of hurt, though I was a bit scratched up too."

Cherry's mouth tightened, eyes lost in a fresh golden brew.

"What did Lana do?" Zinnia asked.

"As I left the scene, I saw Lana merely staring at me, no words. I got in her face, but the bitch had an eerie little smile, very satisfied at what transpired. I stepped back, flipped two birds an inch from her fucking freckles, and went home."

"And you haven't seen Lana Picasso since," Zinnia said.

Jill lifted her pint to Cherry and Zinnia. "Good riddance to bad rubbish."

14

GROUP THERAPY PARTICIPANTS waited for Brian to speak. The long pause was uncomfortable. Ned cleared his throat.

Cherry looked back and forth between heavily breathing Brian and Dr. Grekov. Forgoing her phone, the doctor stared at the rigid man as if a petri dish specimen.

Brian's shoulders jerked. "How come she was so cold?"

"She?" Dr. Grekov asked.

"Mother."

Cherry let out a sigh. Although irksome in his limits of empathy, Brian's brittleness made her frightened for him. It was clear whatever pulsing life he had in himself, it was trapped in a barrier hewn by his mother's rejection. By withholding love, Brian's mom taught him nothing, gave him a life sentence of hurt.

"Why did you seek therapy?" Cherry asked. "You're well into adulthood. I think you're very brave to do so, but I'm wondering why now and...here." She swept a hand in the shape of the Purple Room group seating arrangement.

"My main therapist," a doe-eyed Brian relaxed an iota, "thinks adding group therapy to my treatment is important. My psychiatry costs are already high, and this is free."

"Free because of the generosity of private grants," Dr. Grekov said. "You are on the right track, Brian, even though it will be a long track."

He juggled the air in front of his torso. "It's good, too, because I'm so lonely."

Overcome with sympathy, Ned sank his face into his hands. Tara tsked softly.

Cherry was surprised Brian broke his shell a bit, but his confession saddened her.

"Okay, you're taking a longer turn," the doctor said. "Is everyone okay with that?" Dr. Grekov cleaned her glasses.

Parvati's lips snarled. "Of course! He is so mommy damaged! Go on, Brian."

The counselor ignored her, tapping rust Mary Jane loafers together. "Anyone else?"

"Ah, yeah." Cherry fit her palms onto kneecaps. "Brian, I agree with Parvati. I can't answer to why she would mistreat you. Doesn't matter, she was in the wrong! Period. Like I said, you are so strong to be doing this. And I hope in other parts of your life you are doing whatever the hell you want to feel pleasure."

Still holding his face, Ned spoke through fingers. "Seize the day, Brian."

Chimes sounded from Dr. Grekov's pocket. With the phone muted, she stood and pushed the chair. "The group is making great progress."

"Can I ever discuss my problems, Doc?" Parvati said.

Already inside the door frame, Dr. Grekov half turned to the group. "Parvati's turn next session."

The pneumatic door hissed as it snapped shut.

15

CHERRY FOLLOWED the exiting group members to the door. She held it open, but turned back to see Parvati leaning on the arm of the couch and staring into space.

"Not ready to split?" Cherry returned to the counseling sanctum, sinking into an armchair.

"I know it's free, but I'm not getting my money's worth. Or Medi-Cal's money's worth."

"Yeah, you're right. Who's getting billed? *Alakazam*, no cost."

"You think magic elves do cobbling for Dr. Loafer?"

Cherry busted out laughing. "No, but I love that tale. So, what's the deal with your workplace?"

"My supervisor inspects and criticizes so much. Super nitpicky. I love where I work, my job, but she's making it stressful."

"At least you're employable. Me, not so much. My last boss fucked up my record. He's the one whose crime ring I exposed long after I was terminated." Cherry rubbed her collarbone. "Where do you work?"

"The Exquisite Book and Art Collections Library. My job is to manage a 17th-century European print collection."

"Lofty!"

"Pay is shamefully low. I do get benefits, but don't want to use the mental health part. I want to keep *this* separate from my boss, the director. I don't trust her. She goes through employees—she calls them disgruntled—like toilet paper. And we're always short staffed."

"Does your family help?"

Parvati's brows arched above her square eyeglass frames. "Whoa, this is the group therapy Lidia owes me." She paused to swallow. "My parents are out of the picture."

"Dead?"

With lips locked, she waved "cut" under her chin.

"Touchy subject. I understand. Hey, let's blow Quaking Aspen."

16

ARTUR "BOOP" KULTARIAN waited in the back of the auto-body shop, in a little plant-filled outdoor space designated for smoking and drinking Armenian coffee. The patio was right off a narrow workplace kitchen, a long-handled jezve and demitasse cups on the counter within reach of a gas stove.

The young man paced, jingling metal pieces in his pocket. Brando and Yoke didn't know he was there meeting the chick, the one he mentally called his girlfriend. She had been selling, usually smack, for the crew a long while. Supposedly her dad was high ranking. Artur wasn't sure if he was locked up or dead. He was pretty sure the mom was dead. Or in Moscow. The story was muddled, and he was afraid to ask. *Pussy-whipped*, he admitted, as the sex was always oral, Artur on the giving end, which she held over his head. "Double the globos or I'll tell Brando to smell your breath," she'd say. Yes, a mix of fear and intoxication is what Artur felt for Salem.

Rumble of the street-side utility door rolling shut made Artur's eyes snap to attention.

Stepan, the face of legitimacy fronting Stepan Auto Body, approached, removing and hanging up his charcoal mechanic coat, hairy arms exposed. "Boop, lock up office door?"

Artur nodded microscopically. "Good night."

"Barhi gischeerr," the older man said, the departing call echoing in the cavernous garage.

Artur watched after him, till he heard the motion detector chime followed by a soft thud of the front door closing.

A cartoonish laugh cut the quiet solitude short.

"Tee hee."

Artur about-faced to the patio, long-lashed eyes wide searching for Salem. "Where are you?"

"Up here, dumdum."

Turning to the voice, he saw Salem's face, chin resting on the backs of clasped hands, peeking over the grapevined brick wall.

Artur hustled one of the aluminum chairs to the wall. "What are you standing on?"

"Hood of a car." Salem grasped the trellis, hoisting up to straddle the wall. The skirt hiked up, exposing her supple leg.

Scrambling onto the chair, Artur gallantly offered his arms à la pas de deux to her waist.

Ignoring the gesture, Salem swung the other leg over, cascading to the ground, skirt buoying, revealing a black thong covering her crotch. Artur teetered off the chair.

"You know, that alley would be a good place to dump a body." Salem shook out her limbs and clothes. "Deserted."

With a look of love, Artur attempted an embrace.

"Uh uh, Boops. We need to get the business out of the way." She unshouldered her messenger bag onto the aluminum café table, opening the flap, snapping her fingers at Artur.

He peered into the bag's depths, checking first for anything sharp. During a previous exchange, he nicked a fingertip on an open straight razor. Salem had cackled so hard. With care, Artur pulled out two banded money wads. "So much. Guessing you're inflating prices. You kept your cut?"

"Yes, Betty Boop. Also, I want all the witch this time." Her lean arms rose, deep-purple-nailed hands gathering her dark mane in a temporary high ponytail. "I'm planning a *looong* sales campaign. Could be a while before I'm back."

"Brando won't like it."

"You like my pussy. Brando is your problem. Put whatever's on hand into my bag now."

Strutting to the kitchen, Artur knew he was fucked either way. Opening the icebox, he took out bottles of Ararat Beer, removed the rack, sliding out a false bottom panel. From the hidden space, he extracted a snub nose and two boxes stamped Señor Fiesta, setting it all next to the jezve as he fit the rolls of money into the secret space.

Salem swayed to music playing in her head, swiping the gun, hiding it in the skirt fabric. Boop dumped dozens of filled white balloons and several blue ones into the messenger bag. "Special K," he said, pointing out the blue.

Salem pursed her lips, sucking in cheeks. "Extra special."

When Boop turned to put the refrigerator back together, she put the snub nose into her bag, covering it all with the flap.

Salem backed into the lush vines, gathering up folds of her skirt, exposing the minimal lingerie.

"Okay, Betty Boop. Flutter those long lashes on my skin."

Falling to his knees, Artur crawled to her, eyes dewy with ecstasy. He nuzzled at her underwear.

"Such pretty eyes. Your name should be Betty, not Boop. Look up at me, Betty."

Spellbound, Artur complied, nibbling at the fabric to pull it aside.

The front-door chime rang out again. "Yo, Boop!" called Brando, his and Yoke's shoes scuffling on the concrete floor.

Artur froze stiff, ceasing cunniligus.

Releasing her skirt, Salem hauled one leg over his head, snatched and looped the bag across her body. She placed one monkey boot in the middle of Artur's hunched back, the other boosting onto a shoulder, scurrying up the trellis, over the wall. Once more from the alley side, she popped up her face, flushed with adrenaline, lips swollen.

"Bye, Betty!" she yelled.

Embarrassed, panicked, Artur rose, scrubbed his mouth on a sleeve, and tossed the empty Señor Fiesta boxes over the wall.

17

"NICE NAIL POLISH," Cherry said, sauntering into Quaking Aspen's waiting area.

Parvati held a dog-eared *Helter Skelter* paperback, engrossed. "Top shade is African violet, bottom coat black."

Cherry occupied the next chair. "Light reading?"

"Going through a true-crime binge," Parvati said, a side eye to Cherry. "Right now, I'm only pretending," subtly pointing with her head to a hallway. "Dr. Loafer's losing her PhD composure."

Their therapist clutched the phone against her ear and cheek. "Don't cross me!" Lidia said, face beet red. Then, "Sss...Sss...Svetlana! You'll be the ruin of the family." She looked at the phone, poking it abruptly.

"Svetlana crossed the line," Cherry said under her breath.

She and Parvati shared muffled snorts of laughter. They feigned mutual interest in the Manson Murders book as the doctor cleared her throat to signal the start of the therapy hour. When Cherry and Parvati looked up, Grekov had transformed back into refined Dr. Loafer.

18

"SORRY TO WAKE YOU, Cherry, but Mrs. Cantu is here." Ida nudged her daughter's foot sticking out from under the covers, whispering, "She won't leave till she sees you."

Cherry raised her head. "Hmm. What time is it?" Her phone on the nightstand said 7:30 a.m. "I'll get up."

Ida helped, pulling back the comforter as Cherry maneuvered to standing, PJs kept on. Trudging out of her room barefoot, she spotted Yesenia Cantu, their ultrareligious neighbor, sitting primly on the sofa, skirt tucked around her legs, dogs Yarn and Ball at her side sharing her anxious energy. Esther Lau, their other neighbor, stood in the background shrugging and making exasperated indications.

"Morning, Mrs. C. Morning, Esther. What's up?"

Esther spoke first. "I found Yesenia pacing the sidewalk, in front of her signs, reciting their verses. A little unusual for her. I invited her in my place, but she wants to talk with you, Cherry."

Mrs. Cantu trembled. "Mija, have you heard the news about the niños getting sliced?"

Cherry sat, eyes narrowed.

Her mom sat too. "She means the person planting razor blades at playgrounds."

Cherry's head swayed back at the clarification. "I see. Would you like some coffee? I would." She pointed to the kitchen.

"I would love some," Mrs. Cantu answered, flattening her cardigan as she rose.

Ida got to the kitchen first, commandeering the Mr. Coffee pot. "Can I toast anyone some waffles?"

Cherry raised her hand.

"Café con leche, por favor."

"Esther?"

"Sure."

Once mugs and milk were placed on the gold-specked teal dinette table, disheveled Cherry faced Mrs. C. "What about the news reports?"

"How can anyone be so mean?! So broken?! Un alma basura! El maleficio!"

I'm not awake enough for this discussion, Cherry thought. "We both know what humans are capable of—remember the Errant Sheep Tabernacle, the court trial."

"And you fixed that, mija, my friend. You did a good job helping *those* pobrecitos. Maybe you can help *these* pobrecitos before they get slashed?"

"That's a tall order, Mrs. C. I'm having some trouble sleeping right now. It's hard for me to concentrate on anything. Plus those crimes are occurring in other L.A. neighborhoods, right? That's like looking for a needle in a haystack."

"Not needles, razors."

Cherry took a long slurp of coffee. "Despite being half asleep, I'm with you about that crime spree. It makes my blood boil."

To the table, Ida brought two orange Fiestaware plates topped with waffles. Cherry offered Esther a bottle of Vermont Country Store maple syrup before dousing her own checkered starch disks with amber.

"All we can do is hope the culprit is caught soon, Yesenia," Ida said, patting the wee lady's back. "You're a very caring spirit."

Cherry studied Mrs. Cantu, worrying about her elevated anxiety. She washed down a bite of sweet breakfast, reluctantly acknowledging she had a lot in common with her neighbor.

19

"HOW IS THERAPY GOING?" asked Aviva Krasner, Cherry's girlfriend.

They shared a Mediterranean platter lunch in the living quarters of the Raptor Flats Historical Society and Museum. On Charmany Way off of Sapo Avenue, the offbeat institution was Aviva's ancestral home and residence.

"It has definitely made me feel fortunate," Cherry said. "Except for me and one other person, folks in the group break my heart weekly. They're so fucked up."

"I didn't realize it's group therapy," Aviva said. "I'm sure it's an effective method if you're feeling better."

"Yeah, I get it. What unfolds is relationship issues, struggles, family baggage. Baggage packed with rocks and boulders," Cherry said, holding a falafel ready to eat. "Not sure yet how my sleep disorder will be cured, but, hey, it's free and close by. I did have a more solid sleep last night, but I'm a bit rest deprived. Mrs. Cantu woke me up earlier than I'd like. She had an abstract crisis about the nut booby-trapping playgrounds with razor blades. Have you heard that news story?"

"Mmm. There was a similar case a few years ago," Aviva said, twinging as if sharp pain teleported into her body. "But about the sleep patterns, you have my sympathy. When I was a youngster, my rest times were all turned around after hearing stories about the Holocaust."

"Of course. Heavy for anyone young and old."

"Speaking of violence," Aviva said. "Got a word about the Leibowitz Family Cemetery, you know the smaller of the two Raptor Flats Jewish historic cemeteries. An elderly man was found unconscious at the foot of a 100-year-old grave memorial. It was clear he is a victim of mugging. Visible injuries. He can't recall much of what happened. Whoever did it stole his wallet and valuables."

Aviva paused, eating a pickled beet.

"A grimacing face was drawn in blood on the obelisk," Aviva said in almost a hush.

"Fuckers!" Cherry said, short fuse on fire. "Was it his blood?"

"Probably."

"Good thing he wasn't killed," Cherry said, pressing on with questions. "Jewish?"

"No. Mr. Alexsa Kalevich was visiting interred family in the Serbian Cemetery right next door," Aviva said. "Unpleasant mystery to say the least. So, you were saying there's another group therapy member like you. Not so woebegone."

"Parvati," Cherry said, smiling as she described the scenario with her fun friend. "She's so cool. You're right, she's not miserable at all, though searching for coping strategies. Parvati's quirky, kind of hipster but not. She helps *me* cope with the group and with the blue-blood moderator. We call her Doctor Loafer, due to an interchanging display of expensive shoes. I sometimes chat with Parvati in the waiting area."

"Should I worry?" Aviva said, winking.

"No, no, don't worry!" Cherry said. "You're my number one! Besides I'm not into Parvati in *that* way. Also, she outright told the group she's not sexually interested in women."

"Did that stir things up? That she's so candid."

"Yeah, a little, except for Dr. Loafer," Cherry said. "*That* bitch has a rude habit of checking her phone. Well, can't complain about free. Keep improving, Sleep."

20

EARLY AFTERNOON, Eve's Beer Garden was not yet packed. The tavern with the predominantly female clientele had been open that Sunday since noon. As Cherry and her friends relaxed on the patio, nearby DJ La Vicky—who resembled Peter Pan—spun "Dry Your Eyes," the deep soulful lament by Brenda and the Tabulations.

Zinnia's body kept time with the ballad. "That churchy organ!"

"And the vocals," Jill said, twisting round to mime-flirt with La Vicky, forming a heart with her hands, thumping the shape to the left of her sternum. "Unearthly harmonies." She turned back to the table. "How's your sleep harmony, Cherry Bomb?"

"Improved. Thanks for the gummies. They help. I was sleeping like a log the other day, when Mrs. Cantu showed up to discuss the razor-blade crime spree."

Jill's hands formed a time-out. "Do clarify." The barkeep delivered beers; Jill repeated her beating-heart schtick. "Keep the tab open, please."

"Allow me," Zinnia said. "Someone is planting razor blades on park playgrounds around Los Angeles. I presume your neighbor has fixated on this."

Amid quaffing ale, Cherry danced her eyebrows a few times. "She's worried about the kids getting hurt. Wants me to put a stop to it."

"Oh, oh. That's a lot to expect," Zinnia said. "I've been meaning to ask: When did Mrs. Cantu start putting up religious signs?"

"Sometime after her husband took off, but before her youngest kid left the nest. I think it's why he left the nest."

"I'm glad you keep tabs on her." Zinnia raised an index finger. "About that particular crime, I was called to consult with one of the victims at the hospital. When the injury happened at the park, the accompanying parent was not paying attention."

Cherry and Jill waited expectantly, the latter nodding at Zinnia to spill more beans.

"In this instance, the victim was approached by the perpetrator, a female. And that's all I'm saying."

21

DR. GREKOV WHEELED the chair into the purple group-therapy room. Compared to the dilapidated, mismatched stationary furniture provided to clients, the movable seat was of the expensive ergonomic variety, mesh materials except a plump blue-gray cushion contoured for tailbone support.

As Cherry pondered the comfort disparity, the not-yet-seated moderator began directing the session. "Cherry, what's on your mind?" Grekov sat, smoothing trousers. She adjusted a limb, on its foot a matte-black loafer slide.

Trying *not* to study the shoe's gold chain and designer emblem and blurt out the name *Imelda Marcos*, Cherry closed her eyes and spoke of her decent sleep interrupted by Mrs. Cantu's generalized anxiety about the razor-blade maniac.

"Is she a family member?" asked Tara.

"No, a longtime neighbor."

"Did you want to slap her for waking you up?" Parvati said.

Cherry laughed, then thought about it. "Aside from the dark humor, good point. I wasn't angry. Maybe because I haven't had the dream for a while."

Ned raised a paw. "Seems like the woman doesn't adhere to quiet hours."

"It was only once, and I forgive her. I'm responding to the doctor's prompt is all. We go way back. Though she's a religious fanatic."

Brian cleared his throat, aiming the sound into his collar. "What's wrong with being religious?"

Cherry pulled down the back of her tie-dyed T-shirt and shifted on the sofa to address Brian. "Nothing, Brian. She and I have different world views, but we're friends."

"Different how?"

"Well, my neighbor expresses herself by mounting signs with Biblical messages all over her front yard. I don't."

"It doesn't bother you?" Ned asked.

"I accept it. And she accepts me."

Parvati nudged Cherry. "A win-win. But I'm also curious about this razor villain your neighbor is obsessing about. Does anyone know if the kids were wounded? Their hands or veins? Perhaps the jugular." Under fresh trimmed bangs, her eyes flashed.

Cherry regarded her therapy friend, a little put off by the uncaring, gory fascination. "I haven't heard any reports about specific injuries."

Dr. Grekov tapped the frames of her glasses, speaking with singsong irritation. "Parvati, you're due for a turn. Is this subject pertinent to your reason for seeking therapy?"

Parvati fixed steely eyes on the Quaking Aspen Center director, making squealing, cat-fighting noises.

Brian cupped his pale pink hands over his ears and ran out of the room.

22

BEFORE GOING AFTER BRIAN, Dr. Grekov admonished Parvati for wasting time.

Both Ned and Tara sympathized with Parvati's frustration. "You do get the shortest shrift out of the group," commented Ned as he and Tara departed.

"Maybe this place isn't for you," Cherry told Parvati when they were alone.

The long-haired woman frowned, and her freckled nose crinkled under her glasses. "I know I derailed the talk. Sorry, Cherry. I'm in that true-crime phase still."

Cherry averted her gaze, noticing her fellow client's attire: maroon monkey boots, skinny black jeans, a tee with a small Pennywise peeking out of the pocket. Amused at the subtle clown horror, she thought, *Parvati's odd, Mrs. C's odd, I'm odd.*

"Oddity is not a crime," she said. "Parvati, take advantage of these services. Try loosely applying Dr. Loafer's therapy method. I'll bet your boss is a lot like her."

23

SATCHEL FULL OF BALLOONS, Salem entered the landmark cemetery on foot. Her creepers kicked brown grass, parched blades adhering to her ankle-length ox-blood skirt. While Peter was instructed to be at a gravesite near the center, she took her sweet time visiting a few of the departed.

At the first left rested Academy Award-winner Hattie McDaniel. Under spindly tall palm trees, Salem stopped at the markers of a couple jazz artists before finding the mausoleum containing Tod Browning, movie director of *Dracula* and *Freaks*. Languidly, she traced the engraving of his name and years of lifespan.

Satisfied, she meandered to where that moldy fresa Peter was supposed to leave an extortionate amount of "the root of all evil" in small denominations, encased in a Ziploc, inside the nearest in-ground funerary vase to the right of Maria Rasputin's headstone.

Peter sat against a thick fir tree, looking worried. Salem strutted by, paying him no mind, sitting aside Rasputin's grave. As before, she touched the inscribed words and marker's ornamental bas-relief.

Peter waved to her, softly saying, "Hey." She ignored him,

reclined onto her back, and rolled over the neighboring graves until she found the vase.

Her chin propped by her clasped hands, Salem studied the vase's contents. "There's more black widow eggs here than cash." She snatched the plastic sack, flicking away cobwebs with her fingers. "It's too light." She shoved the sandwich bag back into the vase, still ignoring Peter.

He rose quickly. "Please," Peter said as he approached Salem, now relaxing on her back. "It's all I could scrape up. Please, Salem."

Gazing at the sky, she exaggeratedly twiddled her thumbs. "Did a ghost say my name?"

Peter laughed. "You're clever. No, it's flesh-and-blood Peter."

Finally, her eyes darted at the pale young man. "Blood, you say? From here it looks like you don't have any. Be gone, spook." Salem sat up, making a big show of dusting herself off.

Peter hopped from one foot to the other. "Please, I need a fix."

"You need a fix. I need adequate payment." From a cross-legged position, Salem rose swanlike, skirt unfurling toward the ground. "Where's your kit?"

He patted the left side of his suit jacket.

"By the way, you look and smell like hell," Salem said. "Jackets should be worn over a tailored shirt or at least a nice Henley. You should know that, fresa. That grimy tank top is putrid."

Confused, he looked down at his torso. "Oh, you mean the wife beater?"

Salem's eyes flashed scarily. "Listen, junkie! Do not ever, ever, say that term in front of me. Maybe you should fuck off without your goddamn hit."

Peter shrank into himself, emoting confusion and despair. "Sorry."

Her sneer drilled into him, a wicked grin erupting across her cheeks and freckles. "About that blood you owe me."

Salem opened her messenger bag. Peter's Adam's apple bobbed, his face hopeful. She picked the money baggie out of the vase, dropped it in before rustling deeper. She pulled out two balloons—one white with La Llorona graphic, the other blue. Digging once more, she presented the razor-blade dispenser.

"When you let some blood out for Madam Rasputin, drawing a picture with it on her gravestone, I'll let you have both bulbs. The other catch is, you need to mix them, right now, so I can see."

Sighing and shrugging off his coat, Peter went to work with his wiry, scarred arms. Accepting a razor, he sliced open his left index finger. Sighing louder, he aimed the slight blood flow onto the granite.

"Okay?" he asked.

"Now the picture."

"Fuck. Really?"

"No back talk, dummy."

Peter finger painted a happy face with Xs for eyes, then faced Salem.

"Masterpiece." She tossed him the balloons. "Now part two."

Catching both, he looked around, grabbed his coat and backed up to the tree, sliding to the grass. From an interior coat pocket, Peter took out a military-green sewing kit, unzipping it. Opened like a book, he extracted the tip of a tarnished measuring spoon, a somewhat melted votive candle and a lighter. From another pocket, he took out a water bottle. Setting up operation on a flat dirt patch, he balanced the spoon on the tin of the lit candle, combining powders from both balloons with water into the scoop.

"Muy eficiente." Salem hummed "The Sugar Plum Fairy," waltzing around the blood-stained grave of Maria Rasputin.

When Peter selected a syringe from the sewing pouch, Salem chanted. "Fresa eficiente, fresa eficiente."

He side-glanced at her with a hint of dismay, but never stopped wrapping a sinewy bicep with a wide heavy-duty rubber band, holding the knot with his teeth. With the bubbling solution stirred, he pulled the plunger to suck it up, tapping out air. Choosing an unmarred speck in the canyon of his arm, he shot up.

"Fresa, fresa."

As the narcotic mix effects rained down on Peter, his body succumbed to gravity in slow motion. Salem performed a pas de bourrée around the tree several times, bowing on one knee to slip her bag across her body, resuming the ballet steps offstage, away from the overdosed fresa.

24

"ZIN! OVER HERE!" Cherry waved her friend over to a Ristorante Valenté booth. Grape-bunch lights overhead shined on the table already set with a bread basket kept warm by a red-and-white checkered cloth, along with a colorful vegetarian antipasto salad.

Zinnia slid onto the seat, kissing Cherry's cheek before scooting back, arranging braids behind her. "You're looking better rested! Thanks for ordering ahead of my arrival."

Cherry made inviting hand waves toward the food. "Well, I'm glad you came, 'cause I was about to inhale this plate. Everything okay?"

Zinnia spooned cannelloni beans and red peppers onto a slice of bread. "Yea, just work calls that never stop." She paused to chew with a closed mouth, washing it down with iced tea. "Coincidentally, one was related to the 'razor-blade lady' again. Different kids and families this time."

Cherry clinked down her fork. "What? Can you elaborate? Wait, here comes more of our food."

She and Zinnia smiled courteously as the server brought two plated hunks of eggplant parmigiana and a wish of "bon appétit."

Zinnia dug into her meal, stirring the sauce. "Older children saw a woman hiding things around a park playground. When they looked closer, it was razors. They showed them to a passing jogger who called the police. By that time, the person had disappeared."

"Were the kids hurt?"

"No. I was called because they were out on their own. No supervision."

Zinnia scooped up a few bites. Cherry used the conversation lull to eat more salad.

"A witch is how they described her: dark clothing, long dark hair, laced-up boots."

"You talked with their parents?"

Chewing a mouthful of bread and olives, Zinnia nodded. "Their homes are basically across the street. The parents were shaken and promised to keep better watch."

Looking upward pensively at the grape lights, Cherry played piano on the table's edge. "I swear this happened before. There was a slew of news reports several years ago about razors, glass, nails being planted in parks. I wasn't paying too much attention back then, but it happened in spurts. Maybe not the same person?"

"So much to be worried and anxious about on this earth," Zinnia said. "You're right, I recall hearing about those too. I've got to go. You want to wrap up your eggplant with the rest of the salad?" She signaled to the server.

Cherry leaned to one side, accessing her Care Bears wallet in a cargo pants pocket. "Thank you, I would love the leftovers."

"It makes me happy to see you still using that," Zinnia said, weighing her hand down on the wallet as Cherry tried to pull out money. "But put it away! My treat."

"*Shucks!* Thank you for the meal, and for giving me the wallet ages ago." She folded it back into her pocket. "It makes me feel unique."

Zinnia put a credit card on the plastic payment tray. "'Care Bear Stare!' We were such fans! But! You are unique with or without that wallet, pal."

Cherry blew a kiss. "Wallets and pals, both important in the big bad world."

25

THAT NIGHT AT HOME, after Ida retired, Cherry popped a low-dose THC gummy and searched the World Wide Web.

"Jiminy Hendrix! So many razor-blade incidents. And so many razor blades found by metal detectors!"

She took a sip of water and read on, discovering no arrests happened during the first string of razor-blade planting, though the president of a "moms" club was initially suspected.

"The second spree also happened in Orange County affluent areas. Suspect arrested twice, second time after violating first probation. And SHE tipped off police herself. Hope she found group therapy."

Ball, one of the dogs, came into the room whining.

"One minute, little pooch. Let me finish this article." The piece was from a later date, only two crimes committed in San Diego County, no suspects caught and no incidents occurring after that.

Cherry leaned down to ruffle Ball before heading to the back door, dog following. The other pet, Yarn, shook awake in their donut bed, joining the potty break in the cool night air. As Ball peed and Cherry stargazed, Yarn cautiously approached a Japanese Holly cloud topiary in a dark corner of the yard.

A low growl caused Cherry to notice. *Oh brother, I need to trim that hedge*, she first thought.

Yarn kept up the warning, inducing Ball to join with snarls.

"Girls, come!" Cherry called. The dogs heeded to her feet. "Stay. You don't want to tangle with a raccoon or skunk." She edged toward the plant. "Or a coyote. Stay while I flash some light." Feeling her pocket, she became annoyed not finding her phone. *Shit!* Cherry slapped her hip.

At the sound of the slap, something rustled behind the bush, fence planks jolting about. The dogs yapped anxiously.

Cherry retreated from the area. "Well, I don't want a raccoon encounter either," she said to Yarn and Ball, scooping up one in each arm. "Let's put you goons inside first, then I'll grab a light."

Securing the back door, she ignited a trusty Maglite. Aimed at the corner, the flash created dramatic shadow figures against the wood fence, unnerving Cherry a bit.

She shined the light low, checking for paws, feet or legs. Finding no evidence of a human intruder, she neared the topiary shapes, angling the light through the shrub's recesses. *No skunk coat or raccoon stripes*, she thought, relieved. With her foot, she joggled the bare trunk to scare any critter lingering nearby.

In the corner behind the scraggly domes, she found disturbed dirt. The planks of the fence shared with neighbor Esther were more or less a foot wide. The board at the corner was askew. Squeezing behind the shrub, Cherry poked then pulled at the plank, which opened like a book. *What happened to the nails?* she thought. *An animal could easily pass through here.*

A bat echolocated overhead. She felt the night chill down a few degrees. Yarn yapped at the back door. Cherry about-faced from the pitch corner, vowing to set up a motion-detector lamp and inform Esther about the passageway in the fence.

She bolted the back door, relaxed by interior warmth. The dogs settled in their cushion, Cherry went back to the computer in her room. Whatever roamed into their yard upset her mood despite the earlier pot gummy. Navigating away from the razor-blade news archives, she played a short meditation video and fell asleep.

26

CHERRY SLEPT FITFULLY. As her brain struggled to rest, the specter of the topiary shadows manifested, all made worse by a return of the face-slapping nightmare.

"Good thing it's therapy day," she said to her green ceiling during one of many wakeful moments throughout the wee hours.

Her last stretch of sleep ended close to 8:00 a.m.

"Esther had a prowler in her yard," Ida said, shaking her daughter's shoulder.

Cherry sat up fast, kicking the comforter off and down to the side. "An animal?"

"Human." Ida pointed to the general direction of Esther's house. "Her daughter and the police just left. The cops weren't any help."

Quickly putting on clothes and gargling with cinnamon-clove mouthwash, Cherry rushed next door with Ida.

Mrs. Cantu prayed in the pink kitchen with Esther close by. "Mija," she said upon seeing Cherry. "Is it going to be okay?"

She patted her neighbor's back. "Yes, Mrs. C. Esther, what happened?"

Esther sat at the table. "Veda came by for breakfast before

work. When she checked the backyard vegetables, I heard her screaming angrily, 'Who the fuck are you!?' I ran out, saw someone in dark colors jump the wall while Veda threw a bucket and cucumbers at their behind."

"So Veda could describe them to the cops?" Ida asked.

"Other than probably being a woman, not really. They were sleeping in the pumpkin mounds."

Ida shook her head. "Did the police make a report?"

"Barely. They jotted down what we saw. The clothes too: dark hoodie, with long skirt, bulky monster shoes."

Cherry digested the details, nodding and shaking her head to perk up from fatigue. "Last night, the dogs were growling at our shared fence."

Mrs. Cantu brought her thumbs to her forehead. "Jesus, Maria, José!"

Blinking patiently at Mrs. C., Cherry continued. "And the last plank is broken. I'm going to fix it today, with your permission."

"Thank you, of course," Esther said. "I guess that's life in the big city."

"And in Raptor Flats," Ida said. Everyone, even Mrs. Cantu, chuckled a bit.

27

"MEDITATION IS A GREAT STRATEGY," Dr. Grekov said to Cherry after her turn to talk at Quaking Aspen Center's group therapy. "Even if it wasn't immediately effective. The prowler incident is unfortunate, but you realize it's out of your control." The moderator checked her phone. "Who's next? Brian, go ahead."

Brian scrubbed at his natural platinum hair, skin glowing pink, happy for once to be at the center of the room's attention. "I think I'm in a relationship."

Fellow clients signaled their support. Ned clapped, jovially buddy-punching the air around his denim sleeve. "Good for you, Brian."

Eyes bright, Brian continued. "I started to get notes in my mailbox last week from a secret admirer."

A collective *hmmm* gave way to awkward silence.

Brian pumped his fists excitedly. "Also, flowers and vegetables. Yesterday she left a tiny balloon with a note."

Parvati raised a hand. "You're sure it's a she?"

His face fell into confusion, then he realized the suggestion. "I hope so. That's all I can do, is hope."

Tara chimed in. "If you can feel hopeful, that's an important achievement! I'm happy for you."

Dr. Grekov, attired in pale-green tones, rearranged her crossed legs, flexing her ankle impatiently. "Parvati."

On the sofa, Cherry rearranged herself to better face her therapy buddy at the other end.

Parvati fixated on the doctor's air-peddling shoe. "What color are your loafers?" she said.

Cherry cringed, sensing another contentious discussion.

Ceasing foot movement, Grekov peeked down at her toes. "Reddish brown."

"It's a very specific color, so posh," Parvati said. "More of a sandalwood red, by my arty eye. Pairs beautifully with the seafoam."

For the first time, Cherry saw Dr. Grekov's face infuse with warmth, her eyes soften.

"How's the work environment, Parvati?"

Parvati smiled confidently. "On the verge of improvement." She crossed her legs too, copying Dr. Grekov's position. Cherry noticed flexing of her Frankenstein creepers.

"Wonderful." Dr. Grekov twirled the same foot with renewed vigor. "We've heard some success stories today. Let's strive for more next week." She rose, flashing a grin as she slipped through the exit.

28

CHERRY WATCHED the therapy group members weave out after Dr. Grekov. She remained sunken into the secondhand sofa, alongside Parvati who adjusted her position.

"These cushions. Obsidian would be more comfortable," Parvati said, finally retracting her legs and chunky shoes as if riding sidesaddle.

"Dr. Grekov forgot to wheel her chair out." Wiggling her finger horizontally, Cherry leaned forward. "Was that method acting?"

"Well, sure. I'm trying the method Dr. Loafer, Esquire, is promoting. I regard her like my boss, and I tried speaking to, and complimenting, her interests. Obviously, she's into in her appearance, so painstakingly styled."

"Ha, you've cured yourself. Time for you to bail this sideshow?" Cherry rolled her neck and shoulders.

"And not find out what happens with Brian's girlfriend and brain? No way! His soap opera should win an award!"

Cherry took in her pal's glibness. "Of all of us, he for sure needs our sup—"

The pneumatic door rammed open. Dr. Grekov swept in toward her chair, nabbing the headrest and dragging it like a wagon. At the doorway, she stopped, aware of them on the couch. "An Al-anon meeting is scheduled here momentarily." Detachment had returned to her voice.

Parvati assumed a debutante stance. "Understood," she said, curtsying as Dr. Grekov left.

Cherry laughed at the thick-soled-shoe interpretation of the classical gesture, but sobered quickly, remembering Esther's intruder.

29

IN A MOMENT OF QUIET AWE, soft sunlight poured into the immaculate house. Not a wrinkled rug on the floor, or a porcelain cup out of place.

Cherry gaped at the gleaming-gold thing on the buffet table. A long pipe at the top, like a chimney, handles, a fat middle, and ornate base. She wanted to ask if it was a trophy, but she couldn't speak. A trophy wouldn't have a spout. She wanted to open the spout but was scared to upset the splendid display.

Her view skewed to the right. In the distance, Cherry could see outside a back door a system of tiered fountains and ponds in the manicured yard. She longed to go there to explore, to see the legendary turtles, but permission was denied. She returned to bask in front of the old gilded object passed down from the babushkas.

A voice came from her left. "Cherry." She was scared to look. "Cherry." Turning a fraction, she spotted a blurry figure with dark long hair. Wednesday Addams? Cherry faced the speaker. In heavy silence, the shape moved an arm, waving her to move forward into the hall. She felt reluctance to comply. Cherry returned her scrutiny to the shiny thing from

Russia, the silence muffling out the figure's secretive urgings. That heavy, underwater silence pressured her ears and head. The samovar reflected movement behind her. She didn't turn, paralyzed by the silence. Cherry felt small, nose level with the spout, unseen.

Peripherally, the dark girl figure appeared at her side, reaching for her. A hand grasped her elbow. Immediately the drowning silence gave way to shrieking, godawful thumping, body thuds, pleading sounds in an unfamiliar language. As the figure pulled her to the hallway, Cherry's head wrenched around to see the pandemonium. She saw a shirtless Mexican man, complexion lighter than Cherry's, brutally pulling glossy auburn hair of a European female withering to the knees as he whacked her face.

Her nightmare eyes turned back to the dark hall, yanked by her arm, turning right into a void, hazy Wednesday Addams dissipating, Cherry falling abruptly awake.

30

EARLY MORNING AT RAMIREZ BROS. GROCERY, Cherry was pleased to have the store to herself. As she threw a bread loaf and two packs of lightweight Depends for her mother into the cart, her brain replayed the profound dream.

This time her mind wasn't boggled. Even though it wasn't a clear vision, she knew the shaded presence was her erratic childhood friend Lana Picasso. She realized the dream took place in the Picasso house, and Cherry remembered witnessing Lana's dad abusing her mom.

She woke without incident. *That's progress*, she thought, *perhaps a breakthrough.* When she left the house before daybreak, Ida was asleep. *I feel almost refreshed.*

Eggs, coffee, creamer, apples and a head of butter lettuce rounded out the shopping. Cherry served a helping of po-faced energy to the cashier who commented that she was too old for diapers.

When the automatic exit door swung out, she retreated a foot to grab *The Raptor Flats Siren* from its FREE rack.

Bags in the back of the Honda hatchback, she sat at the wheel, flipping through the advertisement-heavy neighborhood weekly. Bingo listings triggered a flash of bad feelings about the Errant Sheep Tabernacle sex abuse scandal and the notoriety it bestowed on her. Cherry turned to a photo essay about the community garden on Kestrel Lane, across from the "Stuff to Do" section where Aviva's Raptor Flats Historical Society and Museum was featured. Below that was the "Police Siren," a crime blotter for the area.

"There it is," she said. "'Trespassing on the 10 block of Meadowlark Lane, suspect disappeared on foot.'"

Cherry read on.

"'Trespassing on the 20 block of Osprey Road, balloon of narcotics found. Female suspect seen departing on foot toward Los Angeles River.' Same day, maybe same person."

The sun shined through the vehicle windows. Cherry tossed the paper aside and started the engine.

31

FOR WEEKS, Salem had been observing his home, and him. In a dirt alley behind the house, she stashed flower arrangements stolen from memorial parks, and food picked from backyard gardens she trespassed through.

When the man left his modest home one morning, no doubt to go somewhere boring like a job, she had utilized one of many pilfered gift cards to jimmy open a rinky-dink door lock at the back entrance.

Once in, she clomped her boots over well-kept hardwood floors, snooping in dressers and a file cabinet. She laughed at his icebox contents—white bread, boloney, peanut butter, apples, iceberg lettuce—and spat in the homogenized milk carton. At least the freezer had a variety of Stouffer's. The cutlery drawer contained one of each eating utensil, though there was a set of four straight-sided beverage glasses in a cupboard.

Inside a Shaker-style nesting table at the front door was a spare set of keys, one with a Buick logo.

"This is easy," she said, storing the keys in a zippered compartment of her bag. Her laughter echoed in the stark, eggshell-hued living area. She shut up quick, mood switched to bad.

"How come I never had a window seat?" Salem approached a modest picture window in an alcove, sitting on its cushioned built-in bench. The vantage point faced a portion of wall concentrated with framed photos stamped with numerical years. In all of them were two pale, blond parents and a pale, blond boy at incremental stages of growth and development. In each picture the mother figure's face was unsmiling, severe, cold. Expressions of the father and son were compliant but eyes sad, more dejected in each maturing portrait. Pose-wise, the matriarch stood or sat consistently apart from the boy, the husband or a pedestal prop always in between. No embrace, no affection, no connection.

"Little son on a motherfucking prairie," she said. "You'll for sure be my next project."

Realtor promotional pads of paper were stacked near the man's landline phone. Salem helped herself to one, then another, as well as a black Bic pen. She scrawled a note on the blank side of a detached page: U R MY SUNSHINE, decorated with a smiley face sun and swirls of clouds.

Out back, she wrenched open a wood gate to the alley, grabbing a not-quite-shriveled bouquet. She marched through the front yard to a black-metal mailbox at the curb, stuffing in the flowers and note. Salem cackled and singsonged, "Finger of birth-strangled babe."

Another morning, after quite a few days of leaving offerings and anonymous cutesy notes, sometimes at the man's front door, she used the spare key to get into the back seat of his beige Buick LeSabre with beige-palette interior. A sunny-yellow Little Trees air freshener hung from the rearview mirror. "Vanillaroma. No surprise." On the car's floor, Salem hid under an unfurled sunshield.

She heard the front door to the house shut, metallic scraping of keys securing it. Approaching footsteps and more key fumbling. Salem relaxed into corpse pose, willing the fascia throughout her body to melt. *I am Harry Houdini*, she thought. *Without a dick. Or testicles.*

The man entered the car, driver's seat sinking a bit against the sunshield, into Salem's cooked-noodle thigh. The door shut, and he started ignition, driving without much warmup.

The car stereo amplified an easy listening station. Minutes into the drive, the DJ spoke over melancholy piano strains, "Here's Gilbert O'Sullivan's hit from decades ago: 'Alone Again (Naturally).'"

At the end of the first verse, there were burping noises. The car took a left. The burping became coughing. At the song's bridge, lyrics lamenting a plague of broken hearts, the man sobbed while driving. The car didn't stop, continued smoothly, though he bawled, breathing out a series of *whys*.

Salem felt the LeSabre pull into a driveway. The man stopped, putting the car in park. The emergency brake grated, the engine cut, and the radio shut off. The crying and sighing continued for a minute, body convulsions shaking the car seat.

Then he stopped. After rustling of a tissue box and a few sniffs, the man exited and locked the car.

Salem waited a beat. Moving aside the silver shield and crawling slow onto the back seat, she found herself in the lot of an office park, the man walking stiffly into the cavernous mouth of a building complex.

32

AVIVA PUTTERED ABOUT the stove in the centuries-old kitchen of the Raptor Flats Historical Museum. She quickly stifled the water-kettle whistle, pouring a little into a sleek poppy-orange teapot to warm it, before dispensing loose black tea leaves into its mesh infuser, followed by more hot water to steep.

Cherry observed from the breakfast nook. "Is that teapot from Comida Ceramics?"

Comida Ceramics, located next to the museum, was one of the Krasner Family businesses in Raptor Flats, established in the early 1900s.

"Yes, the cups too, like most of my dishes. Manufactured in the 1930s."

"Funny, I've been craving tea since a recent dream."

Her sweetheart brought the now-cozied pot to the table where the matching cups were ready among chartreuse plates piled with cinnamon rugelach cookies and dark chocolates. "Go on." Aviva arranged a cream and sugar set closer to the spread, all the while listening to Cherry's REM description.

"So, no tea was brewing?" Aviva asked.

Cherry laughed. "No. But it's a breakthrough. Besides my PTSD stemming from..." She rolled her hand several times.

"The abuse case."

Nodding with seriousness, she clutched her girlfriend's fingers. "Yes, thank you. As a child, I suppressed witnessing domestic violence in my playmate's house. And my damaged playmate, Lana, with whatever hell she was living through, acted out on me. Slapping me, weird games, like trying to play doctor." She watched Aviva pour the tea. "Ida never knew the details, but she did put a stop to playtimes when she caught Lana hitting me."

Cherry diluted her cup and bit a cookie.

During moments of quiet, the two enjoyed the refreshments. Cherry could sense the wheels turning in Aviva's mind.

"Was there really a samovar in their house? Or was it a dream?" she asked Cherry.

"Yes, there was! Bronze and shiny. I loved looking at it, which wasn't too often. Of course, they were very weird about hosting me, and when I did visit the house—over on Buzzard Drive—I was only allowed in Lana's room. Back then I so wanted to see their fountains and pond turtles."

"Why did they have a samovar?"

Cherry looked up to her third eye, remembering. "Her mom," she said slowly, "was Russian."

"Jewish?"

"Hmm, probably not. I recall baby Jesus icons."

Aviva took sips of tea, savoring it, alternating with small nibbles of chocolate. "Was her dad Russian?" she asked when she finished the candy.

"Oh, no. Mexican. He sort of reminded me of my irresponsible dad, but a real prick through and through. A much bigger asshole." She fixed another cup. "I grew to hate Lana. Her behavior was so toxic, even dangerous. But her family life was fucked up."

Aviva peeked over her cup. "It's a wonder I never crossed paths with her."

"Thank goodness! Again, she was in and out of my life, mostly out since she'd always do something bad to me when we'd periodically rekindle our hanging out. But I do not know exactly what happened to her parents when she went to live with other relatives in West L.A. Or maybe it was the Miracle Mile district. She transferred to a private high school over there, in the Fairfax area."

Aviva put her cup down. "Let me show you something."

Cherry followed her into the old house's preserved dining room. Stopping at an antique hutch, Aviva pointed to a foot-high samovar. Its metal had a matte dark caramel finish, not brassy, and Stars of David at the top and the base.

"Great-grandfather Abraham Krasner carried this from the Old Country."

Marveled by the family artifact, Cherry reacted in hushed tones. "Whoa, it...it's better than the one in my dream."

Aviva opened the glass and pointed to the handles and spigot. "Verdigris patina. I'm happy it's here with me and the museum." As she closed the hutch, the latch clicked. "It's curious, last week a visitor was quite fascinated by it. Tried to open the cabinet!"

"I'm sure you handled them delicately," Cherry said.

"She was an oddball, but compliant. Hardly asked any questions, though she did sign the register twice with kooky names." Aviva rolled her eyes. "It takes all kinds."

"Oddball how?"

"Thrift-shop attire, which I love. Vampira hair but with

bangs. Mod glasses. Creepers or monkey boots...I can't remember. Let's say funky shoes. Not the first goth to visit."

"Veda Lau found someone with a similar description in Esther's vegetable garden, next to us. They scaled the fence. Veda never saw the face." Cherry motioned toward the Dutch door at the museum's entrance. "Can I see the guest book?"

"Sure."

At the registry stand, Cherry ran her fingers down the page of the open book. "Was she the last visitor?"

"Mmm, no." Aviva hunkered over too, grabbing the courtesy pen, pointing with the end without ink. "Here. One line signed Tituba Patel, the other La Llorona."

"Oh, for Christmas sake! What a ding-a-ling." Cherry looked Aviva in the face. "I don't know about Patel, but Tituba..."

"The witch trials."

"Right, and La Llorona drifts among us along the river and waterways," Cherry said. She kissed Aviva's lips. "I'll see you later."

33

"HAVE YOU HEARD?" Ida said as Cherry emerged in PJs from her bedroom.

Still sleepy, she shook no, dropping into a dinette chair, reaching for a brimming mug of fresh coffee.

"An old man was mugged unconscious in a cemetery. And a young man was found dead from overdose in another cemetery."

Sipping caffeine with relish, Cherry blinked her eyes a few times, processing Ida's concerns. "You know, I did hear about that first case. Aviva told me." She mentioned the terrible incident's details, the injured man robbed, left unconscious in one of the Jewish cemeteries, the man's blood used to scroll on a headstone.

"Can't these horrible people leave the dead in peace?" Ida presented her daughter with an everything-bagel egg sandwich. "Makes me want to keep the TV turned off."

"What about our movie nights? And *Kung Fu* reruns among other reality escapes?"

Taking a seat and holding her Yarn and Ball mug, Ida tilted her head. "I mean TV newscasts."

"Today I have therapy. I plan to walk there," Cherry said. "I feel better. What do you think?"

Ida put down her coffee, stood up, and kissed the top of her daughter's buzzed head. "I love you, and I'm glad you're feeling better." She sat. "I haven't heard any fussing from you at night."

34

"ANOTHER SERIAL KILLER?" Cherry flopped onto a Quaking Aspen Center waiting room chair next to Parvati, who closed a book. "You look more like the Unabomber today." She swept her hand over Parvati's gray hoodie, pointing her peace fingers at the sunglasses on her face.

Parvati held up a mass market paperback of *Zodiac*. "Ted Kaczynski was once a suspect." She lowered the glasses to make eye contact. "You look well."

"As well as possible living among the demons on earth." Cherry tapped a finger on the book spine. "Why such a preoccupation on the gruesome?"

Parvati's viewpoint lowered. She thumbed through the pages, removing a black hologram bookmark from the back. As she inserted it where she left off, the image flickered back and forth from a Celtic cross to a snake-holding female goddess. "I think…" Parvati started.

Fellow group member Tara popped her head around the hall corner. "The Purple Room is open."

Cherry and Parvati spoke at the same time. "Hi, Tara."

Tara laughed as they stood and followed. "Everyone's gathered except the therapist."

The only space open was the lumpy couch. Ned waved; Brian nodded, jaw flinching.

"Hello, everybody," Cherry said, sitting. "She's late."

"Doesn't mean we have to wait to speak," Parvati said, looking around the group over her shades. "Folks, right now Cherry asked about my interest in true-crime books. Specifically, serial killers." She presented the garish cover of *Zodiac*, then stuffed it into her messenger bag. "I believe this phase in my reading choices satisfies something. The reports on the subjects and the psychologies tell me we are all vulnerable. Vulnerable in that I could easily be a victim, yes. But in knowing the intimate family histories, I could have easily been such a criminal. The theory here is the family dynamic, right?"

Brian's forehead vein bulged, his face pastier than usual. "Yes."

"Some serial killers' families, it's like, no duh. But others aren't so different from mine, and from what I've heard among us here. Could be a person's roll of the dice, based on chance, the *I Ching*. It's a fine line in taking a few right steps, or bad decisions."

The room was silent, except for Tara crushing a tissue to her nose.

"And in reading these books," Parvati said, "I often remind myself of the fine line and making choices."

Ned stirred, perching at the edge of his seat. "Thought-provoking. Thank you, Parvati. Puts us on a level playing field."

The pneumatic door clunked. The group turned to see the chair glide in with an invisible turbo force. It rolled to a stop behind Ned, the door hissing shut. It opened again, with Dr.

Grekov waltzing in on desert-red mule flats, the buttons of a crisp white shirt of the same hue.

Twirling and arranging the chair as part of the therapy organic shape, she sat elegantly, surveying the group with bored eyes. "Let's start with Tara." Dr. Grekov took out her phone.

35

"TOODLE-OO." CHERRY WAVED BYE to the group therapy participants as she stepped outside.

She veered down Satchel Avenue in the direction of home on Meadowlark Lane. Out of a cluster of bushes, a city path opened to the right. *I remember this walkway*, Cherry thought. The path led to a footbridge scaling an old flood control channel in which Mother Nature had reclaimed some of the concrete space for her flora, as far as Cherry could see. She started up the arched bridge fortified by culvert construction, relaxing at the sight of a stock-still egret, who surveilled a marshy patch of the channel floor. The top half of the flanking safety barrier was chain-link set into a concrete rise. A two-person-wide section sloped toward the canal—as if someone pulled and reshaped the fence while dropping down, perhaps to get to the small camp site Cherry spotted in a dry spot upstream.

At the apex of the bridge, she saw a familiar house, a bit of dread seeping into her chest. It was the onetime home of Lana Picasso, her sporadic wacko playmate, looking unoccupied. From her vantage point, Cherry saw the property's backyard abutting the channel wall, in it the system of turtle ponds, now empty, resembling a miniature skate park.

Descending the bridge toward Buzzard Drive, Cherry briefly let herself feel bad about those unhappy childhood experiences. *Better to acknowledge than suppress*, she thought. *But this park wasn't here when I was a kid.*

Cherry took in the trees scattered around a modest playground opposite the Picasso residence. At the end of the footbridge, when her foot hit the sidewalk, the park came into full view. Emergency vehicles surrounding the green space surprised her. Surprise turned to revulsion at the sandpit tableau.

A dark-skinned boy, elementary school age, held his palms skyward, rivulets of blood dripping between his wrenched fingers. He stood at the bottom of a slide, his mouth an open grimace, frozen in silent scream. At that moment EMTs approached the child, attending his wounds. Another boy, likely his older brother, recounted what happened.

"He went down the slide, and near the end he held the edge. And look!" The bigger kid pointed under the molded plastic. "Razors!"

Cherry halted on the Buzzard Drive walkway, gawking at the grisly, dramatic scene in progress. A distraught woman ran up, screaming, "Mi niño!"

Two TV news vans steered in from different directions. More onlookers appeared. Cherry pivoted around, studying the scene, growing nauseous as the responders transported the bleeding boy to an ambulance, the police cordoning off the area.

The "bad" feeling Cherry had recalled about Lana burned and bubbled up in her throat. She turned to the house, the front yard desiccated and neglected. The proximity disturbed her. The bad force of reported playground incidents had arrived, here in Raptor Flats, spitting distance from the Picasso house of misery.

She looked back at the crime scene.

"Hey," a voice said behind her.

Cherry whipped around, finding a sister descendant of Morticia at the end of the bridge. She sucked in her breath. *Lana?* "Parvati."

Confused, Cherry stammered some sounds, pointing first at Parvati, then the park scene, glancing once at the Picasso home. "Wha...what are you doing here?" she asked finally.

"Driving from therapy, I saw you dart into that cool mysterious route. Because I'm nosy, I parked so I could snoop after you." Parvati lifted her shades. "And this mayhem scene does not disappoint. We're not the only lookie-loos." She nodded toward the crowd widening behind the police tape. "What's the rub? Razor fiend strikes again?"

Cherry's expression became serious, eye daggers aimed at Parvati. "That is what happened," she said after a few moments. "Remarkable guess."

Parvati clapped her hand over her mouth in amazement, a bit of glee mixed in, like she won a prize. "No way!"

"Maybe it tickles your morbid fancy," Cherry said through gritted teeth. "Kids getting hurt ain't my bag."

Her therapy friend looked uncomfortable, then remorseful. "Sorry. I need more filter," she said. "Charm school too."

Cherry's sternness softened. She nodded. "See ya at therapy."

She strode away, around the bulging throng, to the edge of Osprey Road. Turning back toward the bridge, Parvati had disappeared. Looking past that vacated spot, her eyes caught a shadow in one of the windows of the Picasso house. Cherry blinked, refocusing hard on the curtains. "Nothing," she said, continuing the walk home.

36

THE RAPTOR FLATS SIREN

POLICE SIREN

Wednesday: A child sustained lacerations at Buzzard Drive Park where dozens of razor blades were hidden on the playground. It is not certain if this is linked to similar crimes happening around the city. Suspicious activity should be submitted to WeTip.

Thursday: A break-in occurred at Tap O' the Morning Dance Center. There was no theft, but in the studio's practice room, several pairs of tap shoes were found arranged in a circle with human feces in the center. The same day the business installed a security system, as none existed prior to this incident since currency is never kept on the premises.

Friday: A headstone in the historic Raptor Flats Cemetery was vandalized. Caretaker of the graveyard—as well as the Serbian and two adjacent Jewish cemeteries—found the tomb marker of a child deceased in 1909 had been doused in red paint and the grass surrounding it burned. The B'nai Israel Cemetery, the smaller historic Leibowitz Family Cemetery, and the Serbian Benevolent Society Cemetery (where an assault recently occurred) are located north of Raptor Flats Cemetery; all are managed by the Raptor Flats Historical

Society and Museum. Going forward, entrances to each will be locked at sundown.

37

AT EVE'S BEER GARDEN, Cherry's face felt pinched, neck muscles like rock ridges. She remained bottled up with uncertainty about Parvati as Zinnia and Jill chatted up a storm.

"My most recent dalliance gave great head," Jill said. She downed a quantity of ale, then let out a little *hoot*. "If I ever settle down, my spouse would have to be skilled."

Zinnia chuckled. "Priorities!"

"Well, the spice of life." Jill bumped and grinded in her tavern chair. "Amirite, Cherry Bomb? Why so quiet?"

Cherry motioned to the server for another round. When the pints arrived, she took a gulp. "Either I'm a crackpot or the world is one big fucking crackpot."

Zinnia clamped her hand onto Cherry's. "What gives, my dear?"

Drinking more, Cherry took pains to explain. "I have a worry. That my therapy friend is behind the razor-blade spree. You know, sharp objects intentionally placed in playgrounds."

"What makes you think that?"

Cherry recounted the park crime scene on Buzzard Drive. "Therapy ended, we went our separate ways. Then Parvati shows up at this horrific...event. At first, I thought she was

Lana Picasso, 'cause her old house is close by. They look alike. Long black hair."

Jill wiggled again in her seat. "That in itself is bizarro. Doppelgangers." She crossed her eyes, sipped beer, then cradled chin in palm to listen.

"Initially, she was enthralled about the crime and the chaos. You know, there were people gawking and news vans." Cherry tapped fingers on the beer glass, took a gulp.

Zinnia waved a jazz hand. "A spectacle."

"Yes," Cherry said. "I get the observation to a point. But how could she react so removed and unfeeling about the kid? I mean, she saw my disapproval and changed her demeanor."

"It's weird she was there," Jill said.

Cherry knocked on the table. "Right!? It unnerves me. Plus, she's always reading books about true crime and serial killers."

Zinnia whistled softly. "Parvati's not alone in that interest."

"Sure. But the coincidence bugs me. She pushes buttons at therapy, mostly at the therapist, who is literally, actually phoning in her service."

Jill's jaw slacked. "Really?"

"The doctor looks at her phone while the group speaks and supports. Actually, Parvati's helped the folks a lot—she's no nonsense." Cherry finished her beer, motioning for another round. "I'm conflicted. What else is new?"

38

WHEN CHERRY ENTERED Quaking Aspen's group therapy room, Parvati was already there, sitting in what had been Brian's normal seat.

Cherry sunk into the sofa. "How's it going?"

Parvati nodded with a tense, sheepish hint of smile.

"It's going," said Tara from her chair. "How about you, kiddo?"

Cherry looked to a ceiling vent, considering the question. "Adequate. Thanks for asking, Tara." She studied the vent. Something moved on the other side. "See that?" Cherry pointed up. "Something moving."

The two others stretched their heads upward.

"Is it an a/c vent?" Tara said. "Could be air blowing."

The air conditioning shut off, and the shape disappeared.

"It's gone." Cherry clapped, leveling her noggin. "Oh, hello, Brian."

The pallid man hesitated in the doorway, staring at Parvati occupying his usual chair. "Hello." Arms glued at his side, he stepped to the sofa, sitting next to Cherry.

With two fingers, Cherry saluted Brian. "How are you, sir?"

"Me? Fair-to-middling. That's what my dad would say."

"Mine too!" said Tara. "It's wonderful to hear you're somewhat content."

"Never been fair-to-middling before. Suppose it's due to my secret admirer still leaving gifts in my mailbox. And on my doormat."

Parvati nodded impatiently. "What does she leave on your doormat?"

"More flowers. Last week it was a giant wreath." Brian fiddled in a denim pocket, taking out his phone. He showed the group the wallpaper photo, a picture of a funerary spray, a tight bunch of white gerbers assembled as a heart broken by a fault line of blood-red roses. "I think she builds floats for the Rose Parade."

"Or works at a mortuary," said Parvati.

"Mortuary?" Brian looked ready to cry, when Ned entered the room with Dr. Grekov and her chair.

As they sat, Ned spoke. "Well, I've had a shitty week. Someone tampered with my mailbox and broke into my house." He shook his head.

"Mailbox?" Cherry looked at Brian, then back at Ned. "Brian was just..."

Ned continued. "Talk about feeling vulnerable."

Dr. Grekov clicked the heels of dusty-rose shoes. "Yes, let's talk about being vulnerable."

39

"SPECIAL DELIVERY!" someone called outside the front entry, followed by a flurry of marching steps before stomping out the "Shave and a Haircut" tune, kicking the "two bits" part on the door.

Ida approached with care. "Who is it?"

"It's special…" a drumroll tapped on the door surface. "Deeelivery!"

"I'm not opening if you don't identify yourself."

"I'm a ghost. I'm transparent. You won't be able to see me. *Excuuuse* me as I float *awaaaaaay*." The voice became faint, then silence.

Ida waited a few minutes, ear pressed against the door. Certain no one remained on the porch, she flipped the deadbolt and opened, leaving the chain lock intact.

"Flowers." Shutting the door, she undid the chain and reopened. With difficulty, she bent over, picking up a spray arrangement, its roses a little dry. Pulling herself back inside, she secured the entrance, then took a deep breath.

Ida placed the flowers on the Formica kitchen table. She read the sash tribute. "Thinking of you always."

Someone wailed outside the backdoor window. "OOOOOOHHH." Then a hiss.

Looking toward the noise, Ida saw a dark-haired figure darting around.

"What's this all about?" she yelled, startled, hustling to the door. The figure slipped away toward Meadowlark, skipping.

"Damn pranksters," she said, while engaging all locks.

40

"TOO BAD IF YOU'RE UNCOMFORTABLE," Salem told Solomon.

They were sitting in a four door parked on Shrike Place, down the block from Butcherbird Court Apartments. Salem made him pull a hoodie over his yarmulke and locks. Cheap-quality sunglasses pinched from a dollar mart hid much of his face.

"It's your fucking fault for not taking off all those layers of traditional crap. You ought to loosen up, loser."

Hours earlier, Solomon spied Salem standing across the street from his family's grocery store.

"I see and smell you," read her text.

"Go east one block," he replied. "Can't let my family see me with you."

"Duh. That's why you will do as I say."

And now he sat in the dark, in his uncle's car, in the unfamiliar neighborhood of Raptor Flats, an unloaded gun in the bulky hoodie pocket.

"Why are you kidnapping this poor woman?" Solomon said, voice cracking.

"Because I hate copycats who look like me. She can't compare to me and my power. But this little kidnapping is mere fun." A midnight-blue pillowcase appeared from her messenger bag. "The more important reason is extortion, of my cousin, who could get blamed for this." Salem flicked a crimson-and-black peeling fingernail at his face. "Can you say *extortion*?"

She laughed at Solomon wincing, but cut off frivolity when an auto started parallel parking near the courtyard apartments. "Drive to that car now, shithead."

Solomon U-turned and pulled a bit ahead of the vehicle.

"Don't say a fucking peep. Come on." Salem shook the case loose, gathering fabric at the opening as if readying to catch a snake or bag a cat. "Make sure she sees the gun before I sack her."

41

"HELLO, EVERYONE!" Dr. Grekov entered the group therapy room without her rolling seat. "I hope you all had a good week." She sat in a lumpy armchair next to Ned, the one preferred by Brian.

The sofa space next to Cherry was also unoccupied. She exchanged glances of worry with Tara seated to her right.

"So, everybody is okay?" Dr. Grekov asked, forced bright eyes searching their faces for a reaction.

The three nodded, Ned clearing his throat to speak, but the therapist continued.

"I need to inform all of you that Brian is the victim of a crime."

Cherry joined a collective gasp, and Tara clapped a hand over her mouth.

"Is he okay?" Cherry asked.

"He's getting medical treatment. That's all I can tell you. We need to protect Brian's privacy, but I needed to inform the group in case it comes out in the press."

Tara's hands shook. "Is it connected to his mysterious admirer?"

"I can't discuss details any further." Dr. Grekov forced a sympathetic smile.

"This is terrible!" Ned shifted to the edge of the chair cushion, both palms held open toward her in plea. "I mean, last week someone broke into my house. It's upsetting. Can't we talk about this somehow?"

"Actually, due to Brian's situation and other unforeseen matters, I'm cancelling today's session." Dr. Grekov stood, hurrying out the door. "We'll resume next week. Now if you'll excuse me."

Ned and Tara turned to Cherry with miserable faces.

Cherry pointed to the vacant sofa cushion. "Where's Parvati?"

THE RAPTOR FLATS SIREN

POLICE SIREN

Tuesday: Man in coma after narcotic injection. Discovered by passing joggers on the 100 block of Aerie Road parallel to the Raptor Flats Cemetery, the individual was found collapsed over the threshold of his Raptor Flats house, front door open. Police search of the premises found no drugs or drug paraphernalia, and are investigating the incident as a crime, possibly a home invasion. Neighbor statements to law enforcement assert the unnamed man was quiet and straitlaced, never exhibiting suspicious behavior. Authorities are attempting to find and notify the victim's family.

Wednesday: The charitable annex of St. Theodore's Church was burglarized of all gift cards kept in the office. Along with food and clothing, the church holds a weekly distribution of business-donated cards for lodging, restaurants and stores to those in need.

Thursday: A female caused a ruckus outside Acme Descanso Dispensary on Knuckle Avenue. The individual allegedly approached dispensary patrons, offering illicit drugs. Acme Descanso employees including security guards confronted the woman, who hissed and howled at them before running away. After examining security camera images, law enforcement searched the industrial section of Raptor Flats, but found no one matching the person in the footage.

42

BEING A WEEKNIGHT, Eve's Beer Garden was mellow. Nevertheless, DJ La Vicky entertained the sparse crowd with infectious tunes, at that moment mixing in a Nancy Wilson jazz vocal track.

Across from the music booth, a Vampira lookalike fixated on La Vicky, lifting a glass for each song. The DJ smiled at the appreciation, crouching down and digging in her crates to select a record to maintain the atmosphere. When she popped up to play a Mose Allison vinyl, La Vicky found a Visa gift card in her tip glass.

She turned the snifter and squinted at the card attached to its retail packaging. "A hundred?" La Vicky turned about. *Morticia's gone*, she thought. *Better tell Spike.* She motioned to the barkeep, pointing at the gift card.

"Be right there," Spike called.

A song and a half later, La Vicky sensed someone at her side. "Check out this crazy tip form," she said, putting the needle on a record. She straightened, expecting her coworker, but found the mystery goth.

"A reward for your musical curation." The woman moistened her lips. "You've entranced me."

First surprised and confused, she finally nodded comprehension. "Oh, you put in the card. Thank you. But it's too much."

"Can you take a break?"

La Vicky smiled. "No, but my replacement comes soon."

The big tipper pointed toward a desolate group of tavern booths. "I'll wait over there."

A twinkle in her eye, La Vicky nodded, refocusing on the turntables. She snapped fingers to a discotheque instrumental, intrigued by the woman's suggestive actions.

Spotting the next shift's DJ, her friend Cleo also known as Clamtrax, La Vicky put on a Giorgio Moroder extended mix from Eve's LP collection. "I've got a potential good time," she told Cleo, "waiting in a dark corner."

They both laughed.

"Okay if I leave my crate here out of the way?" La Vicky pointed to a container of records in the DJ booth corner.

"Sure," Cleo said, putting on headphones and assessing the controls.

Passing under velociraptor string lights, La Vicky sauntered, searching for the woman, soundtrack beats from *Midnight Express* bolstering her mood. She winked at Spike the barkeep, who waved her over.

"Did you need something earlier, La Vicky?" she asked.

Leaning playfully over the bar, she filled her in about the tip.

"Gift card? Big spender. Let me see."

La Vicky shook her head. "Oh. I forgot it. It's in the beer glass." She glanced around for the woman. "I'll get it later. Right now I'm feeling amorous." She blew a kiss and continued searching the joint for her lucky booth.

Walking deeper into the bar, all the nooks were empty.

Hmm, maybe she bailed. At least I've got the gift card, unless Cleo thinks it's for her. She strolled around the bar. *No dice.* Once more she headed for the deserted, dim booths.

Too bad, these are perfect for making out, she thought, taking a step near a table where there was no light at all. "Better tell Spi..."

La Vicky stumbled over someone's boot. She caught herself before hitting the sawdusted floor, but hands grabbed her ankles from under her. Her head and right shoulder hit the ground. Before she could push up, someone yanked her under the booth's table.

"Spikey! Check out the tip glass." Cleo held up the snifter.

Lifting the bar counter flap, Spike ambled to the DJ booth. "Two gift card tips?"

"Totaling $200!"

"One was dropped in earlier for La Vicky, by some flirt."

Upon the mention of La Vicky, Cleo turned to the booth corner, where her fellow DJ's records remained. "Hey, she never came to pick up her crate."

43

CHERRY ROUSED from an alright sleep to banging on the front door. She and her mother softly collided in the hallway. "I'll see who it is."

Ida uttered, "*Mmm mmm,*" and headed to the kitchen.

"Did you hear?!" Jill yelled as Cherry cracked the door. Jill shook a wrinkled copy of *The Raptor Flats Siren* while crossing the Orozco threshold.

"Are you okay, Jill?" Ida asked, pausing from breakfast duty.

"No, I'm messed up!"

"Sit at the dinette and tell us." Ida resumed brewing coffee.

She sat, slapping the paper hard on her palm. "The girl I was sort of seeing, DJ La Vicky from Eve's, was severely injured. AT THE BAR!" Jill spread the paper wide, pointing at the report. "'The victim, Victoria Espinoza, was found bleeding under a table in a deserted section of Eve's Beer Garden on Tuesday night.'"

"What?!"

Jill read on. "'At this time, Espinoza is under heavy sedation in a local hospital. The suspect is described as a female with black hair, dark clothes and shoes. It seems the suspect left tips in the form of high-denomination gift cards.'"

Cherry mouthed *thank you* to her mom who placed vaporing mugs on the table. "Go on, Jill."

"'A few items were also found under the table alongside the victim: a white balloon printed with a black graphic, a razor blade, and a bar napkin with WRONG PLACE & TIME scribbled in red.'"

A creepy sensation came over Cherry. She felt sick.

Jill went on. "'The last piece of evidence is being tested as the writing appears to be made in blood.' It says the investigation is ongoing, et cetera." Jill put the paper down flat. "I saw La Vicky over the weekend. Lovely person. We were having a good time, nothing deep. Still, I'm in shock. I'm so shaken."

Cherry poured creamer into Jill's cup. "Drink up."

The oven banged shut, flaky biscuits reheating inside it. Ida joined them at the dinette. "About what age is the young lady, Jill? Your friend."

"Hmm. Under 35." Jill thought. "Could be in her late 20s."

"And she's alive," Ida said. "Hopefully getting better every day."

"I tried to visit. No dice. Her room's restricted." Jill's forehead plopped onto her fingers. "I don't even know her family to ask."

"It's scary that this kook is still loose," Ida said. She turned to Cherry. "Wonder if all these weird incidents are connected."

Jill leveled her eyes. "What incidents?"

"Well, the razor-blade fiend, planting razors in playgrounds," Ida said. She tapped *The Raptor Flats Siren*. "Trespassers, like in Esther's backyard. The paper reports on all these break-ins that seem to happen so often. The other day someone knocked on the door, left a funeral spray on the stoop."

"You didn't tell me that!" Cherry said.

"Right after they knocked, I heard whoever it was cackling like a witch at the back door." Ida patted Cherry's arm. "I didn't want you to lose sleep over it. I put the spray in the trash."

Cherry's mouth opened with a mixture of shock and irritation with Ida. She felt a bitchy complaint churning, but out the corner of her eye she caught Jill shaking her head no. "You're thoughtful, Ida. Thank you."

Sipping more coffee, she thought about Brian. "I can't officially confirm this, but," she said, "a person in therapy was victim to a similar ambush crime. The paper, which kept him anonymous, said it was drugs though. No razors."

The oven timer dinged. Ida started to rise, but Cherry got up faster, grabbing an oven mitt. "Description of the suspect bothers me." She extracted the baking sheet, dotted with golden breakfast monoliths.

"Cuz it sounds like Lana Picasso?" Jill asked.

"Well, the thought of that poisonous she-devil bugs me too. Like I told you and Zinnia last time we had drinks at Eve's, it also seems like Parvati from group therapy."

44

NED GREETED CHERRY with a salute. "I think it's just us three and the Doc."

"Parvati is usually here before me, staking claim to the couch," Tara said. "And poor Brian." Her head moved in miniscule shakes. "I expect his healing will take time."

Cherry sat on the sofa, crossing a foot over the opposite knee. "It's weird to be familiar with the group and now two of us are *poof*."

"I feel a loss," Ned replied.

Tara clasped her hands in Namaste. "Exactly. Especially for you, my dear."

The trio's self-help magic broke when Dr. Grekov rushed in, tugging along her chair.

"Seems like you don't need to bring your own seat today, Dr. Grekov," Cherry said, motioning to the open space. "Only three bears today."

The therapist wrinkled her nose, kind of smiling, kind of expressing disdain, sitting in her personal chair. She scanned their faces mechanically. "How is everyone?" The phone appeared from a pocket in her blue-floral pants. "Ned, why don't you start."

"I'm missing our fellow members. According to your guidance, this replicates our family structure. And right now two relatives are absent."

Dr. Grekov's shoulders moved a quarter inch vertically, her head lolling right in a who-cares angle.

"I'm concerned about Brian. It freaks me out that we both had break-ins and I count my blessings I didn't get hurt." Ned aligned wrists on the arms of his chair. "Is Parvati still a part of the group?"

"Sometimes people leave. Part of the process is accepting this."

"It would be courteous to let us know," Tara said. "Has she stopped therapy?"

The room stayed silent for a few beats, Dr. Grekov's eyes on her phone. She looked up as if waking from a nap. "Hmm. Parvati has not contacted Quaking Aspen."

"Have you tried her?" Cherry said.

"That's not our policy."

"But how did you find out about Brian?" Ned asked.

The therapist scrunched apricot-glossed lips. "He...got in touch with us."

"But wasn't he incapacitated?" Tara said.

"All I will say is there was a communication on his behalf."

Cherry fumed at Dr. Grekov. "Aren't you concerned about Parvati?"

Air thick with tension, Tara and Ned waited for the doctor's response.

Dr. Grekov took a deep breath and sighed out an annoyed groan. "The Quaking Aspen Center policy is client privacy must be maintained." The fabric of her wide-leg pants swished as she crossed her knees. "It is also policy that group therapy is a free service. The center owes you nothing more."

45

CHERRY THOUGHT AND THOUGHT. What the fuck is the name of Parvati's workplace?

She scuttled around the house in flip flops, turning toward the window light in hopes it would warm up her brain. "I feel like it was around Pasadena. Pacific Asia Museum?"

Her phone rang out, caller identified as Zinnia. "What's up, Zin?"

"Checking in with the Bomb. How are you?"

"Well…how about coming with me tomorrow afternoon on a museum trip? Can you play half-day hooky?"

Zinnia hesitated. "Hmm. You know, that sounds fun. Sure, let's grab lunch while we're at it. I'll drive."

Zinnia parked in the Pacific Asia Museum lot. "Should we see art before or after asking about your friend?"

Getting out of the car, Cherry stretched. "After." She locked step with Zinnia toward the entrance. "Not sure about the friend part."

At the ticket counter, the clerk directed Cherry to an information desk.

"Is there a Parvati who works here?" Cherry asked the attendant.

The young man scratched his head and hemmed. "I volunteer once a week, so I'm not sure." He picked up a phone. "Let me call upstairs."

Cherry waved Zinnia toward a gallery. "Go ahead, I'll join you."

Zinnia nodded, strolling into the courtyard onto a bridge over a koi pond. She turned back, smiling and giving a thumbs-up to her friend.

Cherry returned the gesture, then faced the volunteer.

"There's no Parvati who works here," he said.

She didn't want to yank Zinnia away from her enjoyment. Yet she wanted to find any info on Parvati. Cherry addressed the young man. "Can you tell me about other museums in the area?"

"Absolutely." From a cubby on the desk, he produced a brochure map. "This also lists the free admission hours of each center."

"You're the tops," she told him.

With museum list in possession, Cherry returned to Raptor Flats with Zinnia. The mind-mending visit let her sleep well. The rest prepared her for a repeat Pasadena trek on her own the next day.

Steering the gold Honda to the 110 North, she paid no mind to admission fees or museum hours.

The first stop was the Norton Simon Museum with a familiar façade. *The Rose Parade route on TV.* She parked in the free lot.

After finding the staff entrance, she approached a counter stationed by a smiling female security officer.

Cherry felt bad making a slight fib. "I'm supposed to meet with someone. First name Parvati, last name escapes me." *At least that part is true,* she thought.

The guard opened a binder with papers in plastic inserts. "No problem. This directory is by first name." As she flipped and regarded the pages, another officer, a burly man, appeared and watched over her shoulder. "Hey, boss."

The man cleared his throat. "What gives?"

"This guest is meeting with a Parvati."

Cherry saw she was in the P section. The supervisor looked at her askance as the woman struggled past the R and S names.

"Could Parvati be the last name?"

Cherry waved the notion away. "Oh, no. Definitely the first name. Perhaps I have the wrong Pasadena museum. But thank you for such considerate help. I hope the management recognizes your hard work!" She tapped the counter surface twice and left.

For the better part of the next three hours, Cherry tried a few other addresses. One was defunct. Another was a children's interactive museum, which she skipped entering.

As she lunched on a #9 Pita Wrap at Zankou Chicken, she surveyed the unchecked museums on the brochure. The accompanying map showed CalTech, as well as the Huntington. *Library, museum AND gardens. Is Parvati's workplace within that joint?*

Like magic, another map icon popped out. *The Exquisite Book and Art Collections Library. Minutes south of here. Better start there before I take a stab at the giant Huntington.* Cherry bussed her tray and left.

She drove south, almost to San Marino, passing a LANDMARK DISTRICT sign before arriving at the address. The structure was a stately Craftsman with vast lawn and a Model T-width driveway at the edge. She parked on the street.

Cherry trotted up to the house's front porch along a ribbon of cobblestone. Deep reddish-brown wood supported frosted glass of the door. Words on a bronze plaque with ringer confirmed the place was The Exquisite Book and Art Collections Library.

"By appointment only," read Cherry. She pushed the button, which generated a string of soaring bongs.

Within a minute, an intercom piped to the porch space. "Sorry, but admittance is by appointment only."

Cherry waved hello upward at the voice. "Oh, can you make a quick exception?"

There was a pause. "The only exception is for representatives from other institutions. We're short staffed."

She stepped to the driveway again, standing with one foot parallel to the manicured strip of grass, punching at her phone.

"Cherry!" answered Aviva.

"Sweetie, I have an immediate favor to ask of you."

"What's up?"

"I'm trying to gain entry to The Exquisite Book and Art Collections Library. It's by appointment only or for other museum reps. Could I act as your stand-in?"

"Absolutely."

"Would you call and clear it for me?"

"Sure, I'll text you when I've contacted the EBACL folks. Come by later and tell me about your scheme."

As Cherry waited in place, her eyes soaked up the

architectural details of the old mansion as well as the neighboring homes.

Her phone lit up: "Lulu is expecting you."

Back at the grand door, she leaned in to ring, but it opened first.

"Your supervisor called. Come in." The spectacled woman swung the door wider and held out her hand. "How do you do, Cherry. I'm Lulu Garcia."

As Cherry shook, she wondered if she needed to pretend official business. She decided to be direct. "Thank you for accommodating me, Lulu. I'm here about Parvati."

Lulu's pleasant face melted. "Parvati? Is she okay?" Her voice dropped low. "She hasn't shown up for days. I thought maybe she's blown off work because she's tired of clashing with the director." She pointed up to the second floor.

"Hmmm. Lulu, I'm worried about Parvati too. I confess, she's my friend, not a professional associate." Cherry took a gander around and up the stairs, then whispered. "Do you have any info you can share with me? Address, phone number?"

Lulu fixated on Cherry's face. "Wouldn't you know that if you're her friend?" She backed away nervously.

"Don't worry," Cherry kept whispering. "I'm not a crook. I just want to find Parvati. It's embarrassing, but we know each other through group therapy, which is intimate, but there are privacy buffers in place."

Listening, the attendant relaxed. "Did she talk about work problems?"

Cherry nodded. "But she stopped showing up. I'm worried because..." lowering her tone even more, "other folks in the group have been victims of crime in their homes. It's a strange and alarming coincidence that Parvati dropped out without notice."

"Geez." Lulu's hands hovered up to her mouth. "Umm, I'd have to get Mrs. Hollingsworth's approval first. Please wait in the parlor." She parted nearby sliding doors with intricate woodwork. Cherry followed, eyes entertained by the lavish "parlor."

"Please have a seat." Lulu closed the doors. The sound of her footsteps elevated up the stairs.

Cherry took in the room's art and décor. "Arts & craft movement," she said, words echoing while sinking into a leather chair with arm rests as solid as boat oars. "I should be smoking a pipe." Wall-to-wall carpet was a pattern of green leafy vines of which the flowers were flames. Portions of the surrounding walls were papered with the same motif. She turned about, counting six tall windows with stained glass vines, as well as six floor-to-ceiling full bookcases.

Muffled voices moved from upstairs to the first floor, stopping at the parlor doors, which spread in a whoosh. The opening framed a woman outfitted in couture. The attire was various shades of gray, except for bright blue driving moccasins. She looked annoyed at Cherry, clicking her tongue, then entering the parlor. Lulu waited in the foyer.

"I'm Mrs. Hollingsworth. What is the purpose of your inquiry?" Her angular silver hairdo framed a hostile face.

"Your employee Parvati is missing, and I'm trying to locate her. Would you be so kind as to give me any contact information you have on file? Anything would help."

"Absolutely not. Now leave."

Cherry's buzzed hair bristled at the scalp. She took pains

not to explode at the cold director. *Better bite your tongue*, she thought. *Parvati's technically still employed here.*

Behind Mrs. Hollingsworth, a sad and worried Lulu mouthed, *I'm sorry.*

Without another word, Cherry walked past the director, nodded sympathy to Lulu, and left The Exquisite Book and Art Collections Library.

46

EXHAUSTED, CHERRY PARKED in front of the Raptor Flats Historical Museum, sitting there a few minutes after turning off the ignition.

She peeled herself out of the car, making her way through the old building's courtyard, stopping to listen to the fountain. Cherry exhaled, then strolled inside, first looking in the Lab.

There Aviva stooped over a vellum document, gazing through a loupe and the archival sleeve.

Cherry collapsed onto a stool at the work table.

Aviva looked up from the eyepiece, smiling. "Hey." She returned her focus to the document. "Lulu Garcia called."

"Lulu? From the uptight Exquisite fuck-off factory?"

"EBACL is the acronym. Rhymes with debacle, to make it easier." Aviva shifted the loupe position. "She gave me Parvati Lespron's info." She straightened, taking a note from her smock pocket, presenting the paper to Cherry. "She's concerned too."

Stunned, Cherry absorbed the note details, first seeing a Raptor Flats apartment address and phone number. "Now I know her last name." Below this was contact information for a Santa Barbara-area location. She shared a look with Aviva.

"I need to send Lulu a thank-you muffin basket. Or a bottle of tequila."

47

"I'M GONNA FUCK YOU UP," said Salem. "I'm gonna cut your hair. Keep your clothes, shoes, and possessions. And why not?" She held up a copy of *Helter Skelter*, using the spine to tap the Cyclops space under her black bangs. "Slice a signature image onto your face." She made buckteeth at her gagged captive whilst removing a wallet from the person's bag with one hand, snub nose in the other. "Sound good, copycat?"

48

AT FIRST, THE MANAGER at the Butcherbird Court Apartments at 23 Shrike Place eyed Cherry suspiciously, after catching her peeking into the window of apartment E.

"I knocked several times," Cherry said. "Been looking for her. I'm concerned."

"There was a prowler pokin' about." The manager receded into her unit at the deepest part of the bungalow-court property, leaving the door ajar. Cherry remained on the walkway between tangerine rose hedges as the woman went on. "Haven't seen Parvati or her car in a while, though I wouldn't be watching out for her so much, since her rent's paid up for six months." The woman reemerged from her apartment with pen and paper. "Funny, that prowler who was sniffin' around? Dead ringer for Parvati from afar. When I got close, I could see it wasn't her and shooed that snoop away. And this one had a nutty look in her eyes. I got the feeling she'd like to spit at me. Gimme your number in case Parvati turns up."

When Cherry recited her info, the woman handed over a business card.

"Give me a jingle when you find her. She's a good tenant."

"Good thing this field trip falls on one of my closed days." Aviva winked at Cherry, then returned her eyes to State Route 1.

"Thanks for driving," Cherry said, looking beyond her partner to the ocean.

Aviva steered off the highway, onto a road bordered by invasive coastal ice plants spreading like The Blob. The GPS guided the car right up a hill, where Aviva U-turned her Prius, wheels adjusted at the curb for incline. "Don't want it to end up in the water à la *What's Up, Doc?*"

"What a flick." Cherry pushed her door open. "Babs stealing the identity of frumpy Eunice Banister. I had the hots for Madeline Kahn."

"Me too." Aviva linked arms as they hiked down to the business set back in an oasis of palms, crunching over a gravel driveway abound with Southeast Asian-style statues and structures.

They walked up wood steps weathered by ocean mist. "About to drop another film reference," Cherry started.

"*The Letter*," Aviva said.

Cherry laughed, propelling them both through an open door.

More figurines—large, small, ceramic, stone, carved wood, Buddha, Ganesha—occupied the inside. Stacked about were display altars of crystals, sacred books, packages of tea, and burning incense, many items dangling with price tags. A few clerks with yin-and-yang name badges hovered over glass cases filled with jewelry pieces designed with the same aesthetic.

The couple meandered through the space, ambient with alcoves and windows revealing a surrounding verdant garden full of ponds, fountains, more idols, and pavilions.

"That famous restaurant, Inn of the Seventh Ray?" Aviva whispered. "This is a retail version."

Cherry whispered back. "Another place to visit someday, but for fun."

They lingered in one room, where two staff persons waited on two well-heeled women. One customer handed over a spiffy credit card, while the other stood inside a circle on the floor as one worker performed a cleansing with a smoking bundle of herbs. The smell reminded Cherry of Catholic mass.

Cherry separated from Aviva, and approached a smiling, white-haired woman with MARTINE printed on her nametag. "Pardon me. I'm looking for a Ms. Lespron."

"That's me. How can I help you?"

"Are you related to Parvati?"

Martine flattened a palm on her clavicle, taking a full breath. "I am her mother."

"Can we speak somewhere privately?"

"Yes." Martine used the same hand to gesture to the staff member finishing the cleansing transaction. "Bliss, will you please bring tea to the Pond Pavilion?"

Cherry followed the woman to a secluded three-walled shelter set amidst ferns. They sat on a cushioned sofa in front of a low table, facing a glassy pond trickling with a bamboo fountain. A sensual bodhisattva figure reflected in the water.

As Cherry described the events that prompted her quest, Martine's eyes, resembling those of Parvati, focused intently. Cherry paused when Bliss slid a high-rimmed tray onto the table, steam rising from two cups.

"A concerned coworker provided me her apartment address as well as this one."

Martine drank from a cup, Cherry copying the action.

"She implied her parents were deceased."

Martine gazed at the remaining tea. "Her father and I divorced when she was a toddler. I joined an ashram, where Parvati was raised. Before she left, she called it a cult." She put down the cup, looking squarely at Cherry. "It was. Parvati rebelled, claimed the leader abused her, and blamed me. I am to blame. When she went to college, she stopped contact with me." She inhaled slowly, exhaled slowly. "I will start the process of a missing person's report tomorrow morning, but it could be brushed off, with our estrangement and the reasons surrounding it." Martine swept her arm the width of their tranquil view. "It's all for Parvati, this lucrative business I established. The land, the assets, the store. I hope she surfaces and lets me into her life again. I want Parvati to know her mother loves her."

49

IT WAS A DEEP SLEEP. But REM itched her brain with a brief dream. Dreamy images really. In a driveway, late-afternoon sun gave off the light that saddens if one is not preoccupied with living, colors muted like an old home movie. A woman held a crate or laundry basket, full of stuff, clothes, standing at an open back door of a compact sedan. The point of view was first close-up, at the woman's side, her face turned away, familiar footbridge in the background. Then her view was from the footbridge, Cherry sensing the channel beneath holding puddles after a rain. The backyard of the Picasso house and its turtle ponds were visible. That was it, what made Cherry awaken, emotional pit of her stomach lurching her body into heartache and sob.

50

"SHOP'S CLOSED!" Ned called out as Cherry approached Quaking Aspen.

Brow furrowed, Tara pulled Cherry by the elbow, situating her in front of the unopen door. Cherry tried the handle; not a budge. Tara pointed at a carelessly scrawled note taped on the inside of the glass:

CLOSED UNTIL FURTHER NOTICE

"A fucking notification would've been professional," Cherry said. "Only three of us to phone."

"It's disconcerting," Tara said. "We depend on this support, at least I do." A nippy wind swooped by them, rattling the door. Tara wrapped her sweater tighter around her ribs. "And presumably all our personal files are in there, in limbo."

Cherry and Ned looked at each other, energized by the same metaphorical lightbulb.

"I haven't seen the intake administrator Carol since day one." Cherry took out her phone, calling the Quaking Aspen number on speaker.

A robot recited, "This number is no longer in service."

Ending the call, she motioned for her support group members to ready their phones. "Time to exchange contact info."

51

SALEM WAS GIDDY, spirits super high, excitement akin to standing at the edge of a cliff.

The grand opening celebration of the new playground at Roasted Park was underway. Wearing a smoky-blonde wig, sunglasses stolen from a kiosk at The Grove, and the busy-bright clothes belonging to that copycat, she stood among the throngs of nearby residents, all facing a podium where a city official spoke into a mic. *Blah blah blah, drink piss*, she thought, containing laughter within a plastered smile, trembling with anticipation. *Blah blah blah, motherfucker.* Salem shifted her weight from one foot to the other, stretching her toes in search of comfort inside creepers.

Hours before, she had done her unique thing: slide, swings and stairs, as well as the jungle-theme treehouse secretly festooned with razor blades, evil Easter eggs set for surprise. "This is *my* thing," she repeated to herself under dark skies, no moon.

When the carnage happened—happy childhood noise morphed to terror shrieks—Salem put on her best face of grief and examined firsthand the bloody casualties. She waited, watching chaos turn into organized mayhem courtesy of EMTs and cops.

When the injured and their parents were taken to the hospital, Salem calmly exited the park. Walking several blocks, she entered a fitness center, flashing a fake member card, proceeding to the locker room where her usual grim clothes were secure behind a padlock.

52

AT 5 MEADOWLARK LANE, Cherry rifled through a pile of unopened mail. "Ida, have you seen these notices from Affordable Healthcare Exchange addressed to me?"

"Yes, dear, but I've been reluctant to bother you about it. Didn't want to stress you more."

Cherry ripped open an envelope. "Your consideration is appreciated. These statements are so complicated. However, it shows that I have had dozens of private mental health treatments, anti-depressant prescriptions, and lengthy visits to a holistic health spa."

"You've been up to a lot. Have you really been using a spa?"

"Nope. This here is fraud, probably identity theft, and a fucking mess for me."

53

VIA GROUP TEXT, Ned and Tara agreed to meet with Cherry at Quaking Aspen to compare similar fishy insurance statements.

Cherry arrived in the parking lot first, sitting a few minutes in her gold Honda, a stack of paper evidence on her passenger seat.

Exiting the car, she checked the center's entry, which now had a padlock and chain binding the door handles. Back in the parking area, she moved toward a medium-size dumpster.

This is a new development, she thought. Sticking out was the lumpy couch from the group therapy space, the Purple Room.

A rattle made the hairs on her neck rise. From the corner of the structure, Dr. Grekov's sacred chair, vacant, rolled toward the dumpster, colliding with its side. Cherry ran to the edge of the stucco building, her good old comfy sneakers crunching over the asphalt of the neglected lot. Peeking round the building, at the other end of the perimeter was someone familiar, with long ebony hair. "Parvati?"

The figure darted away as fast as a squirrel scaling a tree, Rapunzel tresses following.

Cherry took off, dried-rubber of her soles slapping the hardscape.

The one she pursued moved with little sound, except a *squeak* when the thick rubber of their shoes stepped on a manhole when crossing Satchel Avenue, and a *smack* of a messenger bag against a haunch when leaping onto the opposing sidewalk.

When Cherry stepped off the curb, an approaching car honked. She let it pass. Picking up the chase, she heard someone call, "Hey, Cherry, where ya going?" but she pressed on.

Possible Parvati went right onto the footbridge over the flood channel, leading to the old Picasso house and one of the playgrounds of razor-blade infamy.

Coarse hedges scraped her shoulder as she bounded onward. But the chick had stopped, facing Cherry. It wasn't Parvati, but her old nemesis Lana Picasso.

54

"ADMIT IT, MOLDY CHERRY," Lana said. "You've always wanted to French kiss the folds of my asshole."

Cherry grimaced, trying hard to stifle a dry heave.

"It's recently been bleached."

"You bitch. Still the same deranged, horrible Lana," Cherry said, shaking her head.

Lana's ghoulish composure morphed into crestfallen but rebounded immediately. "I'm Salem. You must address me as Salem." She rummaged inside her bag. "Wait, I've got something for you: a plastic dick to cram in your mouth." Salem's hand shot forward, slashing. Cherry darted backward, but a superficial wound appeared on her forearm, vermillion spreading.

Cherry cupped her hand over the cut, steeled her eyes upon her unstable childhood peer, who held an open, bloody straight razor to the sky, pinched fingers ending at many layers of dark nail polish chipped and peeling. Salem stuck out her tongue, shapeshifting into playground bully.

Crouching lower, facing the north side of the channel, Cherry roundhoused her historical foe's midsection. She straightened quickly, took a long stride forward, and back-handed Lana.

Stumbling backward, Lana's eyes were surprised, with the resurrected fear of her child days, of her parents' fighting, when her father's brutality abruptly ended those playdates with Cherry.

But she continued to reach for insults.

"Is that whack in my face your dream come true? Your disgusting shoes belong in the dump, Cherry, you rotten, decaying fruit." She smirked, her cackling echoed off the channel's concrete below. "It's hilarious that you lead a sad, depressing life. Living with your stupid, smelly mom. You should jump to your death, go splat. Get squished."

Banging and muffled shouts from the Picasso house made Cherry look up. Someone—a skinhead?—was knocking their skull against a window. Down in the dry part of the canal a woman, half-full laundry basket balanced on her hip, cautiously approached the bridge.

Lana danced, twitched, gyrated. "Or I can juice you." When Cherry refocused on her, once more the razor was front and center. With a writhing, wide-leg stomp of abandon, she moved at Cherry who then noticed the Frankenstein creepers.

"Lana, is that Parvati in your house?"

The response was a bestial gurgle, low then pitched high as she slashed at Cherry.

Cherry stooped again, under the swiping arm, her shoulders below Lana's torso. She stood rapidly, forcefully. Lana flew, rolling over the rounded, vagabond-modified portion of the chain-link sloping over the channel.

Cherry heard the wet thud. She heard a dual gasp behind

her on the bridge. Ned and Tara stood wavering, their faces stunned and mouths gaped.

The ripped messenger bag clung to a long, solitary fence wire.

From the canal bed, the laundry basket woman called out. "I saw. She tried to cut you up."

"We saw too." Ned's voice rasped, dry from mortal panic. "On the way to meet you, we saw you chasing her as we neared the center."

Sirens sounded, getting louder.

"Now she's cut dead." The women remained in the channel, shaking a phone with the spare hand. "I called the fuzz."

Cherry peered over. Lana was face down, one arm extended, the other twisted under her chest. A pool of blood spread, mixing with water puddles. Lightheaded, she sat on the bridge and looked up at the window. The skinhead's eyes stretched wide and aimed down at the scene, her mouth gagged, a black X on her forehead.

"Ned, Tara. Very sure that's Parvati."

55

THE RAPTOR FLATS SIREN

ALLEGED RAZOR-BLADE CULPRIT DEAD

Former Raptor Flats resident Svetlana Picasso, who in recent years went by the alias Salem, died in a bizarre altercation on the footbridge over Satchel Avenue Flood Channel.

The recent spate of public parks being booby-trapped with razor blades has all been linked to the deceased Picasso. At the time of death, the individual was in possession of several plastic dispensers full of razor blades, along with balloons filled with various powdered narcotic substances, a large amount of cash, and stacks of gift cards traced to a local church burglary.

Picasso is also connected to at least one overdose death, suspected of selling drugs to the deceased. A mysterious assault at a neighborhood bar is also being reexamined as possibly linked to Picasso.

Two clients of the nearby Quaking Aspen Center witnessed Picasso assault a third client with a straight razor. While defending themselves, the assault victim accidentally bumped Picasso over a damaged section of the bridge's safety fence. Picasso died on impact with the concrete channel bed. The weapon was lodged under her chest.

The Quaking Aspen Center recently closed.

Another witness unaffiliated with the center, who happened to be in the channel, corroborated the events.

Complicating matters, it is alleged Picasso kidnapped another Quaking Aspen client, holding them captive in a house next to the flood channel where the accused lived as a child for several years with her parents. The Grekov-Picasso Family Trust owns the house as well as the property where the Quaking Aspen Center operated. Picasso is also the suspect in the burglaries of two other Quaking Aspen clients, and of assaulting one of them. Authorities suspect Picasso accessed the center's files.

In separate but related news, the Quaking Aspen and its director Dr. Lidia Grekov, Picasso's cousin, are the focus of an in-progress investigation for medical insurance fraud.

56

"WHAT A NICE PLACE!" Ned told the Eve's Beer Garden server.

She smiled, nodded, while distributing pints of beer around the outdoor table. Upon presenting Tara with a Snakebite, the server placed an affectionate hand on the mature woman's shoulder. "Enjoy."

Tara sparkled at the attention. "This fun is making me forget I'm going to need a new therapist."

"And how. All of us." Cherry circled her head around. "But let's keep forgetting about that till tomorrow."

Another server brought Ida and Esther Arnold Palmers.

"Aviva, how did you and Cherry meet?" Ned asked.

"She came to the museum looking for Raptor Flats information." Aviva squeezed Cherry's hand.

Cherry relished her hazy IPA, uttering "ah" after each sip, a square bandage visible on her drinking forearm. She faced Parvati at her other side.

"You look good with short hair. We could be fraternal twins."

Though Parvati was frail post-crime, she chuckled at the jab, snorting around a mouthful of ale.

Jill hollered to the server. "I got next round!"

"Howdy, everyone!" Zinnia sang out from the patio garden doorway.

Behind her was Brian. He lifted a wooden hand in greeting, approaching the table.

Cherry swallowed, coughing in surprise. *In all the hoopla, I didn't think about Brian.*

Ned pushed a chair out. "Brian, sit. Join us."

Parvati grinned mischievously.

"How the hell…" Cherry said.

"I went to his place and invited him."

"You know where he lives?"

"Remember how I would joke about him? Well, once after therapy," Parvati said, "I followed him home."

"Why?"

Parvati's face changed to melancholy. "My warped curiosity, nothing more, I promise. No pranks, no harm." Her voice softened. "I'm not as far in the hole as Salem was. May the hereafter treat her better than this world."

Cherry and Parvati stared at each other for a second, their eyes sharing the gravity, the gravity of life's turning points, both wise enough to know the picnic can always be spoiled, but both not ready, or willing, to roll up its blanket.

"The show must go on." Parvati lifted her beer glass, speaking louder. "To Brian!"

"To Brian!" everyone replied.

"And to this good day!" Cherry said.

Glasses clinked, Ned adding, "Here here!"

ACKNOWLEDGMENT

THANKS TO:

Ron Earl Phillips for giving me another shot.

Krissy, Janet, Harry, Peggy, Stacy, Weber, Don and Dan for your genuine insights.

Mr. Jeffrey H. for reading, critiquing, longtime friendship and championing my work.

Coy Hall for his exacting eyes and book boosts.

Melinda R. S. for honest encouragement.

Moe, Calli, Django, Lupe y Moises, Allen and family.

Friends and family who generously $upported the first Cherry Orozco Mystery. I love you all for loving me.

Eric Beetner, Jeff Esterholm, Tod Goldberg, Beau Johnson, Zakariah Johnson, Ed Karshner, Meagan Lucas, Rob D. Smith, Russell Thayer, Mark Westmoreland, Iris Yamashita.

Jens B., Ms. Vaginal Davis, Jennifer L., Kelly M., Loren Q.

The superb authors who gave their precious time to read and blurb this book.

Social media friends who have shown me kindness. As Linus van Pelt said, "Sincerity as far as the eye can see."

ABOUT THE AUTHOR

At three months old, **ILYN WELCH** crossed the USA in a Buick Special with her parents, taking up residence around the aerospace industry in Southern California. A sidewalk encounter with an irate Bob Barker while he taped a segment of *The Pillsbury Bake-Off* began her love for storytelling, which expanded with the public library and television, two dear friends. Ilyn lives with extended family, dogs, turtles and fish in the shadow of a state park.

ABOUT
SHOTGUN HONEY BOOKS

THANK YOU for reading *Bad Makes Bad* by Ilyn Welch.

Shotgun Honey began as a crime genre flash fiction webzine in 2011 created as a venue for new and established writers to experiment in the confines of a mere 700 words. More than a decade later, Shotgun Honey still challenges writers with that storytelling task, but also provides opportunities to expand beyond through our book imprint and has since published anthologies, collections, novellas and novels by new and emerging authors.

We hope you have enjoyed this book, and that you will share your experience, review and rate this title positively on your favorite book review sites and with your social media family and friends.

Visit ShotgunHoneyBooks.com

SHOTGUN HONEY
FICTION WITH A KICK

www.ingramcontent.com/pod-product-compliance
Lightning Source LLC
Chambersburg PA
CBHW011141190726

48289CB00012B/3102